Encounter to Remember

by
KARA LOUISE

ISBN-13: 9798675678402

ISBN-10: 8675678402

Cover images by Dreamstime.com and PeriodImages.com
Cover design by Kara Louise

Printed in the United States of America

Library of Congress Cataloguing-in-Publication Data

Kara Louise
Encounter to Remember

Published by Heartworks Publication

A Note to My Readers

As I prepared this novella for publication, I was ever mindful of the readers who will buy this book and read it. I do hope you will enjoy the story. It is not as long as my other stories, but I hope you will find it just as entertaining.

I wish to thank Mary Anne Hinz and Gayle Mills for their excellent editing skills, and Jeane Tomblin for her final read-through. These ladies have such a way of improving my story, and I appreciate all their suggestions, corrections, and changes.

I also must thank Miss Austen for her great inspiration and coming up with the characters in the first place. They are loved by so many people, and it is out of that love that I continue to write their stories. I hope you will enjoy *Encounter to Remember*.

Chapter 1

The stone walkway leading up to Mr. and Mrs. Gardiner's house glistened with a thin sheen of ice. A few icicles had begun to form and hung from the eaves of the roof. The ice storm that happened suddenly and unexpectedly the day before had removed all vestiges of what had been a warm, budding spring.

Elizabeth Bennet stood gazing out the front window of her aunt and uncle's home and sighed as she looked out at the flower bed where beautiful tulips had just begun to open a few days earlier. They were now encased in a layer of ice.

She cast a worried glance at her aunt. "Do you think your tulips will survive the ice and frigid temperatures?"

Her aunt joined her at the window. "I suppose it depends on how long it remains cold. If the weather warms, there is a slight chance they will continue to bloom." She slowly shook her head. "But if the cold temperatures continue, and the ice does not melt, they very likely will not survive."

"I hope the other flowers you have planted will still bloom." Elizabeth shivered as a draft of cold air penetrated her wool shawl.

Mrs. Gardiner took her niece's arm. "Come, let us sit near the fire where it is warm."

They settled into comfortable chairs, and Elizabeth stared into the fireplace watching the flames frolic and dance. She placed a coverlet over her lap and smiled as she listened to them crackle and pop.

"At least we have nowhere to go today," Mrs. Gardiner said as she took a sip of tea. "It is certainly nice to be able to stay indoors and not have to venture outside in these conditions."

Elizabeth tilted her head. "But tomorrow... You and Uncle

Gardiner must go for the final fitting for your new clothes. What if it is still icy? It would be hazardous conditions in which to travel – or even walk."

Her aunt drew in a long breath. "We have a little time if we must wait. We do not need the new clothes until two weeks from Saturday. If it is too treacherous outside tomorrow, we will have to make another appointment."

Elizabeth smiled. "It is best to be safe."

"Yes," her aunt agreed. "It is always best to be safe."

~~*

Elizabeth stood at Mrs. Gardiner's side at the London dressmaker's shop. The weather had finally warmed up, and they had waited an additional day for most of the ice to melt before venturing out. There were still small patches, but it was not as bad as it had been.

Mrs. Gardiner tried on her dress and was delighted it only required a few minor alterations. Elizabeth and her aunt looked through bins of lace, buttons, and ribbons that would embellish the gown while Mr. Gardiner sat in a chair reading the newspaper. He wanted nothing to do with the decisions that were required for the gown, apart from how much it would cost him when it was finished.

There was nothing he disliked more than being fitted for a new suit of clothes. He had put it off long enough, however, and could come up with no reasonable excuse to delay it any further. He had recently put on some weight, and his clothes were now fitting too tightly – if at all. He restlessly squirmed in the chair as he waited for the ladies to finish. He had already been next door to the tailor's, tried on his suit, and was glad to be done. He was grateful men needed few embellishments, other than a fine neck cloth and a handkerchief.

As Elizabeth waited for her aunt to finish, she walked to the window and looked out onto the cobblestone street. She enjoyed watching the crowd of people bustling about, and all the carriages, gigs, chaise-and-fours, and phaetons that paraded up and down the street. The vendors selling their wares called out to the people as they walked past. She loved the busyness and the liveliness that was found here, although she knew if she lived in London, she would likely long for the peace and quiet of her country home and neighbourhood.

She had come to London for a brief visit with her aunt and uncle. She had so enjoyed the time she had spent with them the previous summer traveling to Derbyshire that she immediately accepted the opportunity to visit them again when they invited her and Jane.

Jane was not to come, however. Mrs. Bennet had adamantly refused to permit her to leave, as a rumour had begun spreading about Meryton that Netherfield was being prepared for its resident to return. Despite the unreliable source of that rumour, she insisted her daughter remain at home to be available if Mr. Bingley happened to return and call at Longbourn – which she was certain he would do.

Elizabeth let out a long, soft sigh. She knew the likelihood of Mr. Bingley returning was poor, and it was more probable that the home was being readied to be shown to other interested parties, or perhaps it had already been let to another. She strongly doubted that Mr. Bingley would return after being gone for more than a year.

Noticing a small bookstore across the road, she turned back to her aunt. "Would you mind, Aunt, if I went to the bookstore across the way?" She tilted her head. "It will only be a brief visit. I am certain you do not mind." She gave her aunt an encouraging smile, hoping she would allow her to venture across the street and visit the shop by herself.

Mrs. Gardiner arched a brow. "With anyone else, I would insist you wait for me to accompany you, but as you are my independent and stubborn Elizabeth, yes, you may. Cryderman Bookstore is an excellent store and has a great number of books." She raised her brows. "Do you need any funds?"

"No, I have a little in my reticule."

"I will be finished here shortly, and if you have not yet returned by then, I shall join you."

"Thank you, Aunt Gardiner. I hope I will find something of interest."

"Take care and watch for any lingering patches of ice," Mrs. Gardiner called as her niece stepped out the door.

Elizabeth set out across the road, carefully dodging the carriages and eluding the men selling their wares. She noticed there were still some patches of ice here and there and was careful to step over or around them.

As she walked up the steps to the store, she could not help but think of Mr. Darcy's library at Pemberley that she had seen while in Derbyshire. Her hand went up over her heart as she recollected the beauty and vastness of it. She had secretly wished she could have been a little mouse and hidden away to live in it the rest of her life.

She let out a giggle, which quickly softened to a moan. "I would not have to wish to be a mouse if I had only accepted the man's offer." She paused as she placed her hand on the doorknob and entered. "But I did not, and at the time I had good reason!"

She gave her head a shake and stepped in. The smell of the small bookstore was heavenly. There was something about the smell of leather book covers, a variety of papers that made up the pages, and stained wooden shelves that now held the books. As she looked around, she saw that it was smaller than Mr. Darcy's library. It was likely this little bookstore did not have as many books as he had in his own library!

"Good day, Miss." A blond-haired woman stood in front of the counter, handing what looked like some food to the gentleman behind the counter.

"Thank you, Susan," the gentleman said as he brought a piece of bread up to his nose and sniffed it. "Ah! There is nothing like the aroma of freshly baked bread."

He looked over at Elizabeth. "Welcome to Cryderman Bookstore, young lady. I am Mr. Cryderman. Is there anything I can help you find?"

"Thank you, no. I think I would just like to look around first," she answered. "If you do not mind."

"Be my guest." He pointed off to the side. "Our newest books are on the table there. Please let me know if you need assistance finding something particular."

Elizabeth smiled. "Thank you. I certainly shall." She looked at the fire blazing in the fireplace. "It is delightfully warm in here." She laughed. "Much warmer than outside!"

"That it is," Mr. Cryderman said. "If you think you will be here for a while, feel free to hang your cloak up on the rack at the front."

"Thank you, I believe I shall!" Elizabeth slipped the cloak off her shoulders and hung it up.

As she walked to the table of new books, Mrs. Cryderman leaned in towards her. "If you enjoy good fiction novels, they are along the back shelves. Let me know if you would like a recommendation. I have read many of them and have my favourites." She turned her head towards the gentleman. "My husband has his favourites, as well, but they may not be suited to your taste."

"Thank you. I shall look at them directly!"

Mr. Cryderman turned his attention back to his freshly baked bread, and his wife began straightening up some books that were placed on the front table. Elizabeth turned towards the back shelves. As she did, she saw a gentleman step out from behind them. Her heart leapt when her eyes locked with Mr. Darcy's!

Chapter 2

No sooner had Elizabeth comprehended Mr. Darcy's presence than it appeared he noticed her, as well. He gave a slight nod of acknowledgement towards her and immediately moved back behind the shelves.

She came to an abrupt stop, her heart pounding. He had certainly seen and recognized her. Her mind was beset with thoughts and questions as she pondered what to do. He most likely did not wish to see her. She ought to turn around and walk out of the shop, or she could peruse the shelves in the front of the store and then leave. Her feet, however, seemed disinclined to do her bidding, and she unwittingly took a step forward.

He had given her a brief nod, and she recollected it was much like the one he had directed at Mr. Wickham when the two men encountered each other in Meryton. She knew how he felt about *that* man, and Mr. Darcy now likely felt the same about her, considering their last encounter. Her foot took another step forward.

Oh! Their last encounter had been disastrous! His proposal had been brash, demeaning, and so unexpected! Her refusal had been so much worse. She could barely recollect the words she had lashed back at him, the accusations she had hurled at him, and the names she had called him in her refusal of his suit.

She still had time to turn around and walk out of the shop, but there was a tugging deep within that tried to convince her to do otherwise. He had been in her thoughts almost daily since first reading his letter back in Kent. As she had walked through his home in Derbyshire and heard the highest praise of his housekeeper, Mrs. Reynolds, her heart had softened, and her feelings towards him had begun to improve. She took another step. The floor creaked beneath her.

Her heart pounded fiercely with each step as she drew near him. It beat with the same ferocity as it had when she had walked the halls and into the rooms of his home. She had been so fearful of encountering him, yet at the same time, she felt an inexplicable hope that she would. She had greatly enjoyed seeing the rich splendour of Pemberley.

Her foot unwittingly took another step as she considered her only regret that day had been not being able to tour the grounds, as it had begun to rain. They had subsequently left with only a view of the beautiful grounds from inside the carriage.

She heard Mr. Darcy place a book back on the shelf, and she took another step forward.

Would he consider her impertinent for approaching him? Was his retreat behind the bookshelf due to his not wanting anything more to do with her? Was she being foolish to even consider walking up to him? She could barely think, let alone direct her feet. They seemed to move without any prompting from her, and she could not bring herself to stop and turn around, as she ought.

She took a deep breath, stepped past that last bookshelf, and watched as he gently pulled another book from the shelf. He turned his head, drew his shoulders back, and straightened when he saw it was her. She perceived a small intake of breath, a slight twitch of his lips, and finally, another slight nod.

"Miss Bennet."

Elizabeth dipped a curtsey. "Mr. Darcy." She attempted to smile, but whether it was perceived by him to be genuine or forced, she could not know.

After a moment of awkward silence, Mr. Darcy spoke. "What brings you to London, Miss Bennet?"

"I am visiting my aunt and uncle. They are across the street having a final fitting for some new clothes they are having made."

A barely perceptible smile appeared. "And you could not resist coming to a bookstore unaccompanied?"

She tilted her head and gave him a wide, genuine smile. "Yes. As my aunt claimed, I am stubborn and impertinent to even consider doing such a thing. You know me quite well."

He was silent for a moment, his brows lowering. "In some ways, perhaps, however in other ways..." He gave his head a quick shake and quickly turned his gaze back to the shelf of books.

Elizabeth cast her eyes down, and her fingers clutched the fabric of her dress. She, who loved to sketch a person's character by observing their facial expressions, the tone of their voice, and their posture, could discern nothing that would indicate how he felt about seeing her again. She had never been able to judge him accurately! Was he perturbed by her presence or enjoying it? Or worse, was he altogether indifferent about seeing her again?

There was silence again for a moment, then he turned back to her. "When I saw you just now, I... I stepped back, as I was not certain you would want to acknowledge me."

Elizabeth took her time to answer, realizing he had stepped back for *her* comfort, and not so much for *his*.

"Yes," she said slowly, "I can understand why you might be under that... *misapprehension*." She held her breath for a moment as she watched for his comprehension of what she meant. She detected a slight raised brow.

She continued. "I am... pleased to have encountered you, for I..." She shook her head to gather her thoughts. "Mr. Darcy, I feel as though I must apologize for my words and actions when we last saw each other in Kent. I was misled, deceived, and completely mistaken about you and your character." She paused and cast her eyes down. "As well as someone *else's* character."

Darcy drew in a breath. "I feel it is incumbent upon me to apologize to *you,* Miss Bennet. I was unfeeling, unkind, and could not have behaved more unforgivably to you in my... in what was supposed to have been a declaration of my hopes and feelings."

Elizabeth heard the quiver of emotion in his voice while noticing the struggle to maintain his composure reflected on his face. She wished with all her might that she could reach out and take his hand. She smiled, instead. "It seems we both behaved badly that day." She smiled. "I certainly accept your apology and ask that you please accept mine."

Every line and muscle in Mr. Darcy's face softened at her words. "Indeed, I do most readily accept yours."

She gave him a nod of appreciation. There was silence again between them, until Darcy suddenly pulled out his pocket watch. He quickly pocketed it and looked intently at her.

"Miss Bennet, I fear I have an appointment with someone, and I must take my leave directly or I shall be late. Would you... I would be honoured if you – and your aunt and uncle, of course – would be my guests at Darcy House tomorrow. Do you know if you have any plans? I leave the day after to return to Pemberley, so tomorrow afternoon would be the only time for a visit."

Elizabeth could feel the pulsing of her heart from her head down to her toes. She was astonished that he would extend to her such a courtesy and honour by inviting them to his home after everything she had said to him. She felt her cheeks warm, but she looked up with a smile. "We have no plans, Mr. Darcy, and I believe I can speak for my aunt and uncle. We would be delighted."

He replaced the book he had been holding back onto the shelf. He pulled out a card, as well as a pencil, and wrote something on it. Here is my card with the address. Will four o'clock be acceptable?"

"Yes, that would be ideal."

"Good. He wrote something else down and handed it to her.

Elizabeth reached out for it and felt his fingers brush her gloves. She shivered and felt her cheeks warm. She silently debated whether to tell him of her visit to Pemberley a few months back but quickly decided against it – at least for the moment. She would wait until tomorrow when her aunt and uncle were with her.

"Thank you," she said.

"Until tomorrow, then." He gave a slight bow, and then a smile appeared. "Four o'clock."

Elizabeth quickly nodded as he turned and walked away.

"Did you not find anything to your liking, Mr. Darcy?" Mr. Cryderman asked as he approached.

"Not this time, Mr. Cryderman." He suddenly stopped and turned to look back at Elizabeth. "At least, I did not find what I came in for. I wish I could stay longer... to look around more... but unfortunately, I have an appointment. I shall stop back in when I return to town in a few months."

"I am certain you will find something then. There are always new books coming in."

He said goodbye to the owner and his wife and walked out the door. Elizabeth looked down at the card, his printed name and address on one side, and on the other, he had written '*Four O'Clock, Until then,*' and then signed his name. She ran her fingers over the even letters. The pencil lead smeared slightly, but his penmanship still looked neat.

As she looked at his name, *Fitzwilliam Darcy*, she was suddenly taken back to the morning after he had proposed. He had gone out specifically to meet her, and when he encountered her, he handed her a letter. She had initially decided against reading it, but curiosity and a desire to affirm her accusations against him had prevailed.

Just as now, she had been struck by the neatness of his hand. Miss Bingley had been correct in her assessment of it. It was not just the neat, even strokes of his writing that had instantly impressed her as she had read his letter, but the open and articulate manner in which he had defended himself to her.

She slowly walked back to the front of the store, keeping her eyes on the card as she did. When she reached the front of the store, she looked up. "Thank you. I must return to my aunt and uncle, who are across the street being fitted for clothes. You have a lovely store, and I look forward to coming in again in the future."

"I hope you will do that," Mr. Cryderman said.

"And be sure to ask for me if you do," Mrs. Cryderman added with a smile. "I can give you many good recommendations."

Elizabeth thanked them both, retrieved her cloak, and stepped out.

As she gazed back down at the card, her hand began to shake, and she grasped it with her other hand to still it. She let out a small breathy laugh as she considered what had just occurred. She would never have believed, when she had been walking through Pemberley last summer, that an encounter with him would be so pleasant.

After their tour of Pemberley and hearing the praise of his housekeeper, her aunt had declared that he had to be a fine gentleman. His own father had been highly esteemed by the people in Lambton, the small village where she had grown up, and she was convinced he must be, as well.

Her aunt had heard her speak of her initial dislike of him, but Elizabeth had never mentioned his unexpected proposal and her subsequent refusal. As she had read and reread his letter, and then later as they toured Pemberley, her feelings towards him had begun to change for the better.

And now... she felt... could it be?

Elizabeth pinched her brows slightly as she tried to recollect what her aunt had told her and Jane several years ago when they had asked her how they would know whether they were in love with someone. She bit her lip as the words slowly came to mind.

"You know it is love," her aunt had said, "when you catch the twinkle in his eyes but cannot catch your breath; you feel a blush in your cheeks, and your knees feel weak." Elizabeth sighed. She had just experienced all those things, but the last line evaded her. She knew there was one more part.

She turned back to look at the bookstore, and a smile suddenly came to her face. "Ah, yes! Your heart gives a shudder, and your mind is in a flutter, that is when you know it is love."

She laughed, nodding an affirmative to those two traits, as well. She glanced down at the card one more time before placing it into her reticule. She took a step as she turned around, but suddenly, she found herself sliding. She flung her arms and tried to regain her balance, but the patch of ice refused to give her a firm footing. She looked about in horror as she grasped the air for something to hold onto. There was nothing she could do. She let out a cry as her feet twisted beneath her. Her foot crumpled down the step, she hit her head on the stone wall next to the walkway and fell limply to the ground.

Chapter 3

The following afternoon Mr. Darcy paced about the study in his town home, feeling as nervous as a young schoolboy about to ask a young lady to dance for the very first time. He gave his head a brisk shake, trying to gain at least a semblance of calm and control as he awaited the four o'clock hour, which was intent upon taking its time.

He occasionally gave a tug of his coat or loosened his neck cloth, each action followed by a long huff. He finally sat down in a large chair and stretched out his legs. He contemplated what this afternoon might bring and rubbed his chin as he did.

"Heavens! I am more uneasy than when I went to ask..." He paused and leaned his head back. "Perhaps if I had felt more apprehension when I asked for her hand, I would not have approached her with such an absurd assurance that she would undoubtedly accept me!"

"Fitzwilliam?"

Darcy looked up to see his sister standing in the doorway. "Georgiana. You have come." He stood up and walked over to her.

"You said it was urgent. Is something wrong?"

Darcy pinched his brows. "No, nothing is wrong."

"Good. I am glad to hear that all is well."

He took her arm and brought her into the study. A nervous smile appeared. "But whether all is well will only be determined in the course of a few hours."

Georgiana tilted her head. "I am at a loss to understand you. You say there is nothing wrong, yet all may not be well?"

She sat in the chair next to her brother's, folded her hands in her lap, and looked at him quizzically.

"We have guests who will be arriving shortly."

"Oh? Who?"

Darcy drew in a breath. "Miss Elizabeth Bennet and her aunt and uncle."

Georgiana opened her mouth but seemed unable to speak for a moment. Finally, she said, "Miss Elizabeth Bennet? The lady you came to admire in Hertfordshire?"

He nodded silently.

"How did this come about?"

Darcy smiled and sat down. "I stopped at Cryderman's Bookstore yesterday to see if I could find anything of interest to read."

"And?" Georgiana inquired, when he paused and drew in a breath.

"I was in the back of the store looking through the books, and when I stepped out from behind the shelf, I saw her."

"Miss Bennet?" she asked with a smile.

Darcy turned his gaze toward the window as he recollected the moment his heart began pounding when he saw her. "I felt..." He chuckled. "I felt a jolt of something. I know not if it was fear, elation, or a combination of the two. And then I was at a loss to know whether I should greet her or step back behind the shelf."

"What did you decide to do?"

Darcy moistened his now dry mouth. "I acknowledged her with a nod and then stepped back."

"You did not greet her warmly and eagerly? This is the one woman whom you found to be truly delightful!"

Darcy swallowed hard, looked down, and began to slowly shake his head. "There were some things I neglected to tell you..."

Georgiana pressed her lips together and then said, "You stopped writing about her in your letters shortly after you encountered her in Kent. I thought you... I thought perhaps you had decided she was not suitable."

Darcy pushed himself up from the chair and walked to the fireplace. Looking down into the glowing embers, he began rubbing his chin. "On the contrary, she was everything suitable for me." His brow furrowed. "However, in some ways I had considered her unsuitable. I struggled with it." He slowly turned. "But any unsuitability was diminished by her liveliness, her intelligence, her beautiful eyes, and..." He paused.

His sister's eyes widened. "And? I am eager to hear what else you found admirable in her."

Darcy looked up and a small smile appeared. "She never catered to my opinion; she had the courage to disagree with me on several occasions and on several subjects."

Georgiana's brows shot up. "She disagreed with you, and you found that to be an admirable trait?" She smiled. "Perhaps I should add that to the list of accomplishments I need to practice?"

Darcy scoffed. "On the contrary. But when every woman a man meets continually agrees with all his opinions, he might find it refreshing to meet a young lady who has no qualms to express what she truly thinks or believes." He lifted a brow at his sister. "Even if it is a contrary opinion."

"I see. But what happened in the bookstore?"

Darcy drew in a deep breath. "Before I get to that, there is one more thing I never confided to you. While we were in Kent, I asked for her hand..."

Georgiana clasped her hands. "Did you truly?" Her eyes suddenly narrowed. "But you are not engaged..."

He swallowed hard. "No. She refused my offer of marriage."

Georgiana hurried over to her brother and wrapped her fingers about his arm. "Oh, Brother, I am so sorry." She looked up at him, compassion written on her face. "What happened? Why did she refuse you?"

He drew in a deep breath. "It appears she believed me to be proud, ungentlemanlike, and she told me that I was the last man she could ever be prevailed upon to marry."

Georgiana gasped. "No! How could she have said such things? How could she have such an erroneous opinion of you?"

Darcy covered his sister's hand with his. "In some ways she was right, but in other ways she had been deceived..." Here he paused and looked at Georgiana. "She had been led to believe some lies about me. I was able to clear those up, but..." He pressed his fingers to his forehead and began to massage it. "She was right about several other things."

"I do not understand! How could she think that? Why do you say she was right?"

"I had behaved abhorrently in the neighbourhood where she lived and where I felt completely ill at ease. I had interfered in something where I should not have, and it distressed her immensely." He slowly shook his head.

"But Fitzwilliam, she is coming today." Her face lit up in a smile.

"Yes. To my surprise, she walked back to where I was standing. We had a very amiable conversation. I can only hope that today I will have the opportunity to tell her how I have since taken her words to heart and hope to redeem my character in her eyes."

"I am certain she will see what a good man... gentleman... you are!"

He smiled, but it quickly faded. "Georgiana, I have never met her aunt and uncle. I do not know whether they are..." He stopped. "No, it is of no import."

A puzzled look crossed the young girl's face, but she soon smiled. "Brother, I know that all will go well with her visit. I cannot wait to meet her!"

He grasped her hand. "I am looking forward to you meeting her, as well."

~~*

Darcy paced the floor in the parlour as he watched the hand of the clock on the mantle move past the four o'clock hour. One minute... two minutes.

He grumbled. "It is not unexpected that they might be a few minutes late." He glanced out the window. "Possibly there is still some ice that is slowing their travels." He raked his fingers through his hair. "If only my racing heart could comprehend that!"

Georgiana peeked in. "Have they not yet arrived? Are you faring well with the wait?"

Darcy forced a smile. "As well as can be expected. Mrs. Holbright, however, is ready to order me out of the house, as I keep checking with her to make certain all is ready for our guests."

Georgiana stepped in and sat down. "I am certain she is not! She is the kindest person with whom I am acquainted, and other than Mrs. Reynolds, the best and most loyal of housekeepers." She chuckled. "And extremely patient with you. She always has been."

At that moment, the housekeeper tapped softly on the door. "Everything is ready for your guests. Let me know if there is anything else you need."

"Thank you, Mrs. Holbright. It appears all I need now is for them to arrive."

Georgiana folded her hands in her lap and tried to smile. "You see? She is not at all vexed with you. And I am certain your guests will be here any at any moment."

As each minute passed, however, Darcy became more agitated. He would sit and start tapping his fingers on the arm of the chair one moment, and then would stand and begin pacing the floor the next. A huge sigh filled the room, and Georgiana tentatively looked up at him.

"Perhaps something happened. They may have encountered some ice, or some situation occurred that prevented their being able to come."

Darcy sat down, resting his elbows on his legs. "Or perhaps she only wished to not hurt my feelings in the bookstore by agreeing to come and never had any intention to do so."

Now it was Georgiana's turn to sigh, her shoulders drooping. "Oh, Brother, you do not believe that. I cannot imagine that a woman whom you so admired would resort to such a ploy."

"But no note? No apology for having to cancel their plans to come?" He stood up again. "I am going to be in the library... if they happen to come." He started to walk out and then turned. "Please advise Mrs. Holbright to preserve any of the refreshments that will not spoil, and if they have not arrived by five o'clock, to send them out to the street urchins. I hope *they* enjoy them, for *I* certainly shall not!"

In the sanctuary and solitude of the library, Darcy felt the weight of disappointment descend upon him. It was as if he was living anew the pain of rejection he had suffered almost a year ago. His mouth grew dry, and his stomach ached for food. Yet he could not eat. He poured himself some brandy and took a few gulps as his eyes travelled to the clock. Five o'clock. He was now certain they were not coming.

He called for his valet. He would be departing on the morrow for Pemberley and could think of nothing that would soothe his bitter spirits more than to leave London and not look back.

When Warrington stepped in, Darcy inquired, "Is everything ready for our departure tomorrow?"

"Yes, sir."

"Good. I would like to leave no later than seven. I am considering riding Chalice so I can make better time. You may ride in the carriage."

"As you wish, sir."

When Warrington left, Darcy leaned back in his chair. He looked over at the mail on his desk, determined to do something other than wonder about Miss Elizabeth Bennet. He picked up a few pieces and then tossed them down. He found it difficult to concentrate on anything.

He called for Georgiana. When she arrived, he bade her to come in and sit.

"You have heard nothing still, I assume?"

He gave his head a brisk shake. "No, and I doubt I will. It was all a misunderstanding." He clenched his jaw. "It was likely my hopeful thinking that misinterpreted our conversation."

"Whatever it was, Fitzwilliam, I am terribly sorry. I would like to have met her."

"You know I am leaving for Pemberley on the morrow. I plan to depart early and will be riding." Darcy's shoulders rose as he took in a long breath.

A sly smile appeared on Georgiana's face. "The horse's pounding hooves will certainly drive away your melancholy." She looked down, and then lifted her eyes. "I would suspect the slow, solitary ride in a carriage would only serve to torment your thoughts about Miss Elizabeth Bennet."

Darcy lifted a brow. "Yes, you know me too well." He suddenly thought of how Elizabeth used those same words in the bookstore. He thought he knew her well, but for her failing to appear without sending a missive explaining their absence did not seem like the Elizabeth he knew.

"I know you will find the peace you need at Pemberley."

"I hope you will be able to join me shortly." He smiled faintly.

"I look forward to it."

Darcy looked up eagerly as Mrs. Holbright stepped in.

"Excuse me, Mr. Darcy, but before I give away the food as you requested, I wanted to check with you, first. Do you still want me to do that?"

He forced a smile. "You and the staff may have a share in it, but then give the rest away."

"Yes, sir. Thank you. I shall take care of it. And Mr. Warrington informed me you will be riding on the morrow. Would you like me to pack some food for you?"

"Fruit and bread should suffice. I will stop at some inns along the way if I get hungry."

"Yes, sir."

"Oh, Mrs. Holbright, one more thing."

"Yes?"

"If I receive any personal mail here, please have it sent directly to Pemberley."

"Yes, sir."

Darcy turned back to Georgiana. "You see, Georgiana? I am giving Miss Bennet an opportunity to explain herself."

Georgiana tilted her head. "But will she not feel it improper to send a letter to you?"

Darcy looked down, letting out a soft laugh. "If she does, she can always have her aunt or uncle pen the letter."

"I do hope you hear from her. There must be a logical explanation."

"I do not know whether I hope to hear from her or not. I suppose it depends on what her excuse might be for not coming."

Georgiana reached up and kissed her brother's cheek. "I shall leave you now. Farewell, Brother. Please take care, and I will see you in a month."

He squeezed her hand and then released it, watching her walk out the door.

He pondered Elizabeth. Would she consider it improper to write to him when she had once accepted a letter from him? He shook his head as he thought about some aspects of her behaviour that one might consider improper! She took walks alone, even three miles in the mud to see her sister at Netherfield. She spoke her mind not only to him but also to his aunt. He could not prevent the smile that appeared. "She walked into a bookstore in London unaccompanied!" While that memory of their encounter and conversation in that bookstore filled him with elation, her failure to come to his home after saying she would, filled him with great anguish.

Chapter 4

Elizabeth struggled to open her eyes, but quickly closed them again as pain and confusion overwhelmed her. Her arms flailed about, and she cried out. "Where... where am I? Mother? Father? Jane, are you there?"

Mrs. Gardiner gently cradled her niece's hand within hers. "I fear that your parents and dear sister are not here. This is your Aunt Gardiner, dearest Lizzy. You have been injured, and as a result, you have had a high fever." She called out to her husband, "Edmund, bring some tea! Elizabeth has awakened!"

Elizabeth closed her eyes again, more from the pain shooting through her foot and head, than trying to comprehend her aunt's words. She heard heavy footsteps draw closer.

"She is awake?" Her uncle's commanding tone and her aunt's comforting presence brought her a sense of calm, even if she did not fully understand what was happening.

"Yes," her aunt said. "She briefly opened her eyes and spoke to me."

"That is a good sign." He began to gently brush away some hair from his niece's forehead. "Can you hear me, Elizabeth? Can you hear us?"

Elizabeth's eyelids were heavy, and she struggled to open them again. "Aunt?"

"Oh, Lizzy, how good it is to hear your voice!"

Elizabeth brought her hand up and gestured towards her mouth. "Thirsty..."

"I am pouring you some tea, Lizzy."

Mr. Gardiner carefully lifted her shoulders and head up as his wife brought a cup of tea to Elizabeth's lips.

"Here you are, dear," Mrs. Gardiner said. "Take some small sips. We have not been successful getting you to swallow any liquids. This will help."

After taking a few sips, Elizabeth felt more able to open her eyes fully. She looked about her. "I am in your house, but this is not... my room."

Mrs. Gardiner grasped her hand. "Your room is upstairs and would not do. It was easier to get you into this room."

Elizabeth shook her head and closed her eyes again. "Everything seems to be a blur. Did something happen? I really cannot remember anything."

She heard her aunt sigh. "Edmund and I went to be fitted for some new attire. You accompanied us. Do you not remember?"

Elizabeth slowly shook her head. "I am sorry."

"There is no reason for you to feel sorry, Lizzy. You had quite a blow to your head."

She brought her hand up to her head and felt the bandages. "I took a blow to my head?"

"You fell and hit your head," Mrs. Gardiner said softly. "No one saw you fall, but we assume you slipped on some ice."

A puzzled look appeared on Elizabeth's face. "Ice?" She shook her head. "How could that be? The last I remember was looking out your window at the tulips in the garden." Her eyes widened. "How long ago did this happen?"

Her uncle clicked his tongue. "It has been three days. We had an unexpected ice storm here. It is still spring, the tulips are still in the garden, but I fear they may not fare well."

"Oh, Lizzy, we thought most of the ice had melted when we went out, but apparently there was still a small patch of ice on the steps of the bookstore." Her aunt's soft, soothing voice reassured Elizabeth.

"Bookstore?"

Mrs. Gardiner patted Elizabeth's hand. "Yes, you went to the bookstore across the street while we were having adjustments made to our new clothes."

"We believe you slipped on the ice and fell. You suffered a fairly severe head and foot injury."

Elizabeth tried to wiggle her toes and winced. "That is why I am in so much pain." She lifted her brows. "From my head... to my toes." She tried to laugh, but instead grimaced.

"Yes, dear," her aunt said. "Your foot has a slight fracture, or so the physician believes. He did not perceive a broken bone from the feel of it, but he will know more once he talks to you. He will have a better idea of the extent of the injury by asking you about the pain and then seeing how you do when he moves it around and you put some light pressure on it."

"He has wrapped it tightly so whatever the extent of the injury, it will not worsen," her uncle added.

"How could I have been so careless? What was I doing that I did not notice the ice?"

"We may never know, Lizzy." Mrs. Gardiner grasped her niece's hand. "Fortunately, Mrs. Cryderman, the bookstore owner's wife, came and found us after it happened. You had told her we were across the street. She said you had just stepped out of the store when they heard you cry out."

Elizabeth let out a moan. "How foolish of me! I wish I could remember something of that day! I do not recollect anything." She suddenly looked up at her aunt and uncle with wide eyes. "Have I been asleep ever since I fell?"

She noticed her aunt and uncle look at each other. "Yes, Lizzy." Her uncle leaned down to kiss her. "We have been waiting patiently for you to awaken."

"Your mother and Jane are on their way," her aunt assured her. "They left Longbourn this morning. We... we encouraged them to wait a few days, hoping your condition would improve before they arrived. We know how much your mother worries, and her nervousness may not have aided your condition."

Elizabeth's brows narrowed. "Are my injuries that serious?"

Again, her aunt and uncle looked at each other. It was her aunt who spoke. "It was your head injury that concerned us most. Fortunately, the physician was able to examine your foot without having to worry about any pain you might experience. But with a head injury... well, we are greatly relieved you have awakened."

Elizabeth closed her eyes. "I feel terrible that my carelessness, however it happened, caused you and everyone else so much concern."

"There is no need for that, Lizzy."

"I wish..." Elizabeth began ruefully, "I wish I recalled... something of the events of that day."

"Well, now all you need to do is rest. You will need all your strength when your mother arrives."

Elizabeth let out a long sigh. "At least Jane is coming."

"Yes," her aunt said. "Jane is going to be tasked with minimizing your mother's nerves and removing her from your presence if she becomes too agitated."

Elizabeth smiled. "Yes, Jane will prove to be very useful in that regard."

Mrs. Gardiner patted her niece's hand. "You rest now, dear. I will send a missive off to Mrs. Cryderman at the bookstore and inform her that you have awakened. She was terribly worried and asked that we kept her informed of your recovery."

When her aunt and uncle stepped out of the room, Elizabeth closed her eyes. Despite her fatigue and pain, she began to move her foot around, wincing as she did.

"Oh, dear, I hope it is not broken," she said softly. "I cannot imagine not being able to take my long walks anymore." She shook her head. "And why is it that I can remember nothing of that day?"

~~*

It was a few hours later that the carriage carrying Mrs. Bennet and Jane pulled up in front of the Gardiners' home. Elizabeth had been sleeping and heard the commotion when her mother entered the home.

"Where is she? Where is my Lizzy? Does she still have breath in her?"

Elizabeth could not discern the quiet responses of her aunt and uncle, but she assumed they were reassuring her mother that her daughter was still among the living.

She braced herself for her mother's dramatic entrance and was not surprised when she stepped into the room, exclaiming, "Oh, my Lizzy! I thought I would die of shock when I heard what happened! Whatever were you thinking? Were you not watching where you were going? But you are awake! We are all of us delighted!"

Jane stepped to the side of her bed and leaned over and kissed her. "Lizzy, it is good to see you. It was wonderful to be greeted with the news that you had awakened."

"Yes, it is good to be awake, but I fear I do not have any memory of what happened. I cannot even recollect going out with my aunt and uncle that day."

"Oh, dear!" Mrs. Bennet exclaimed. "But you do remember us, do you not? It would be dreadful if you did not recognize your own mother!"

"Yes, Mother, I only have no memory of that day." She let out a soft laugh. "Perhaps it is better that I do not recall what happened."

"Yes, I suppose, but I would like to know how it happened!" Mrs. Bennet shook her head. "I would not be surprised if the shop owner was negligent in keeping his walkway free from ice!"

"Now, Sister, I do not think he was," Mr. Gardiner assured her.

They talked for a while, and then Elizabeth yawned. "I own that I am fatigued. Would you mind terribly if I ask to be left alone so I can take my rest and, perhaps, sleep?"

"Oh, certainly!" Mrs. Bennet said.

Elizabeth extended her hand. "But Jane, you will stay, will you not? I would sleep much better knowing you are at my side."

Jane smiled. "Of course, if you wish it, Lizzy."

Mrs. Gardiner took Mrs. Bennet's arm. "Come, let us go have some refreshment. I am certain you must be hungry after your trip." She looked back as they walked out. "Jane, would you like me to bring you some refreshments?"

"Thank you, no."

When they stepped out, Elizabeth closed her eyes. "It is so good to have you here, Jane. I am not so much tired as I am in need of some peace and quiet with you by my side."

"I am here," she replied. "And I shall remain silent."

"No, you must tell me what has been happening at home." Elizabeth let out a soft laugh. "I have missed everyone and am eager to hear news of Hertfordshire."

Jane smiled. "I am not certain how I am to be quiet and speak at the same time."

Elizabeth reached over and took her sister's hand, giving it a squeeze. "Your voice will be very soothing to me. You must tell me all that has been happening."

"There is not much to tell," Jane said softly.

"Is Father prepared to keep Mary, Kitty, and Lydia in tight reins while you and Mother are in London?"

Jane chuckled. "I think I saw him trying to put a lock on his door to the library so he would be left in peace."

Elizabeth smiled, closing her eyes as she did. "That would not surprise me in the least! If that is the case, I hope he has Hill keeping an eye on the younger two." She moved her leg and winced in pain. "I need to remember not to do that."

"I am so sorry." Jane moved some strands of hair off Elizabeth's forehead. "My, you feel warm."

"I have had a fever, but I believe it is improving."

"I am glad of it."

"Jane, tell me how Kitty and Lydia are doing. More particularly Lydia. I assume Mary is still Mary, but does Lydia still maintain her story about what happened in Brighton?"

"She does. She insists she confided in Mrs. Forster about Mr. Wickham's plot to sneak away with her because she knew it was wrong for him to do so."

"I still wonder if that truly was Lydia's reason in confiding in her," Elizabeth said softly. "But whatever her reasons were, it was fortunate she chose to confide in Mrs. Forster."

Jane murmured an affirmative. "And even more fortunate that Mrs. Forster chose to confide in her husband!"

Elizabeth silently nodded.

It was a moment before Jane continued. "He has been found, Lizzy."

"Who? Mr. Wickham?"

"Yes, and with all his debts in Meryton, Brighton, and others he accrued along the way, as well as deserting the army, he likely will be imprisoned for many years."

"Well, I hope so!" Elizabeth said. After a moment of silence, she asked, "How did Lydia take the news of his capture?"

Jane folded her hands. "Surprisingly well. At first, she seemed astonished and somewhat concerned, but any feelings she may have entertained for him soon vanished. She insisted that he was getting what he deserved and was grateful that he would be paying for what he did."

"Mm. I am glad to hear Lydia feels that way. I own that I often wondered whether she apprised Mrs. Forster of his plan to leave with her with the sole motive to boast to her of his attentions. Then when everyone turned against him, she decided to claim she had informed her so Colonel Forster would know that he was about to desert."

"I would like to think that she knew better than to run off with him."

"As do I! But enough of Wickham. Tell me, Jane, is there any other news in the neighbourhood?"

Jane gave a shrug. "Nothing of which to speak."

Elizabeth opened her eyes and lifted a brow. "You cannot mean that. You must know I want to hear whether Mr. Bingley has returned to Netherfield. That was the reason you remained in Hertfordshire, as there were rumours circulating that he was returning." She smiled. "Has he come back with the sole intent to show you particular attention again?"

Elizabeth watched as Jane lowered her head.

"Oh, Lizzy, I fear it was just a rumour, and not a reliable one. He has not returned, and there is no further talk of his coming any time soon."

Elizabeth took her sister's hand and squeezed it. "I am sorry you have had to endure the rumours and speculation."

"It has been over a year since he left Netherfield. I cannot believe he would choose to be gone this long and still have any intention to return."

There was silence between them, and then Jane asked, "But how are you, Lizzy? How do you feel?"

"I confess that when I awoke earlier today it took me some time to comprehend where I was. And it was disconcerting that I have no memory of what happened."

"Well," Jane said as she patted her sister's hand. "I am just grateful you are awake."

"While I am still fatigued, I believe just your presence here has given me a little boost of energy." She chuckled. "Please do not inform Mother."

"I promise!"

"You had best return to her and Aunt Gardiner. You may need to rescue our aunt from Mother."

"She is always so patient with her," Jane said.

"Yes, but there is a limit to her patience."

Jane leaned over and kissed Elizabeth's forehead. "I shall leave you to rest. I love you, Elizabeth, and am so grateful you seem to be on the mend."

"Yes, I am grateful, as well. I cannot help but wonder, however, how extensive my injuries are, and..." She paused.

"Yes?"

"I wonder if I will ever remember anything that happened that day."

Chapter 5

The Gardiners' physician, Mr. Chester, came to check on Elizabeth the following day. With Elizabeth awake, he was better able to ascertain the extent of her injuries by the pain she experienced and her foot's mobility.

He gently pushed and prodded, while Elizabeth tried to relax. With each move, twist, and pressure applied, he asked her to report to him how her foot felt, how much pain she suffered, and how long the pain lingered.

When he finished, he crossed his arms. "I do not believe the bone is broken, for I do not feel any sort of break. It is more likely you have a slight fracture, and possibly an injured Achilles tendon. That would cause a good amount of pain." He felt around the foot again. "There is still a lot of swelling, so there is some sort of injury."

"Perhaps I merely twisted my ankle?"

"I believe it is a little more severe than that."

He advised her to stay off her foot for at least a month to six weeks, and then to begin walking on it only when she felt little or no pain.

"Shall I be able to take my long walks again?" Elizabeth asked. "Will I ever return to normal?"

"It will all depend on you and your tolerance for pain," he replied. "If there is some small fractured bone in your foot or if the tendon is damaged, it will likely produce pain when you walk — especially if you go on long walks." Mr. Chester let out a huff. "If you are inclined to walk a great distance, especially uphill, I would advise you to always have someone with you. If there is a fracture, a small piece of bone may dislodge and move, causing such discomfort that you would find it difficult to take even a few steps. But a slight fracture can heal with time, so that is our hope."

"And if it is my Achilles tendon?"

He crossed his arms in front of him. "You rely on your Achilles tendon with every step you take. You use it to point your foot downward, rise up on your toes, and then push off again." He shook his head. "I fear your gait may not be as elegant as you would like." He looked down and smiled. "I cannot stress enough the importance of keeping your movement to a minimum."

Elizabeth swallowed hard and felt a great sense of discouragement. "Yes, Mr. Chester. I understand." She looked at her aunt with a smile. "I imagine this means there will be no dancing at Almack's for me."

"Or anywhere else," the physician added. "At least for a while. You, along with the pain you experience, will be the best determining factors of what you can and cannot do."

"Thank you." Elizabeth gave a slight nod.

She was disappointed in the restrictions he gave her, but grateful there was hope for a full recovery if she did as she was told.

As he was about to leave, Elizabeth called out to him.

"Mr. Chester?"

"Yes?"

"What about my memory? Will I ever remember what happened that day?"

He inclined his head. "Do you really want to remember?"

She shrugged. "I suppose I do. I want to know how I could have been so careless."

"Well, young lady, I cannot guarantee that your memory will return. Just be grateful your memory loss seems to be of such a short period of time. With the head injury you suffered, your total memory could have been lost, and you would have no idea of your identity or that of your family. I have seen much worse."

Elizabeth shuddered and thanked him. She could not imagine losing her memory to such an extent. At least it seemed she had lost only the day the accident happened.

As the physician prepared to leave, he spoke with the others, informing them what he had shared with Elizabeth.

After he left, they came into the bedroom to find Elizabeth seated on the bed, with her legs over the side.

"How are you feeling, Lizzy?" Jane asked.

Tears filled Elizabeth's eyes, and she let out a sigh. "I suppose I should be grateful that the injury was not worse. I hope it will heal completely. I just cannot imagine not being able to go for my long walks anymore."

"Lizzy, I never thought a lady should be out walking alone – especially climbing up some mountain, as you do Oakham Mount!" Her mother shook her finger at her.

Elizabeth gave a resigned shrug and glanced down. "I suppose walking up Oakham Mount is now out of the question."

"Maybe for just a short while, Lizzy." Jane gave her an encouraging smile.

She looked down as she wiggled her foot, wincing as she did. "It is hard to believe that an injury to one's foot would result in such a prognosis."

Her aunt reached out and took her hand. "Lizzy, you had a bad fall. We have to be grateful that it is as minor as it is, despite its limitations."

"Yes," Jane added. "Let us be grateful that it was not more serious. I know I am."

Elizabeth looked up and smiled. "I know, and believe me, I am, as well. I truly am."

~~*

There was one more visit from the Mr. Chester before he allowed Elizabeth to travel home to Longbourn with her mother and sister, with her agreement that she would take care and do everything he advised. She was to rest and continue to stay off her foot, not putting any pressure on it for a few more weeks. She was not to do anything that might aggravate it or make it worse.

On the day they were to leave, Elizabeth said goodbye to her aunt and uncle and their children, giving each an appreciative hug.

"Thank you so much for the opportunity to spend time with you and for taking such prodigious good care of me!"

Mrs. Gardiner seemed reluctant to release her niece from her hug. "It has been our pleasure! I only wish –"

"Do not even say it, Aunt," Elizabeth interrupted, shaking her head. "The accident was entirely my fault. I may never know what I was thinking or doing to have been so distracted and careless, but I do not want you to blame yourself at all!" She pulled back. "Do you promise?"

Her aunt gave her a weak smile. "If you insist, Lizzy, but I still wish I had not let you go across the street to that bookstore alone. I should have insisted you wait for us to finish, and we could have all gone over together."

Elizabeth sent her aunt a pointed look. "Aunt Gardiner, please do not conjecture what may or may not have happened if you had done or not done one thing over another."

Her aunt smiled and gave her another hug. "You take care, Lizzy." She inclined her head. "And promise me you will take care of your foot."

"I will, Aunt. I promise."

~~*

Darcy had been at Pemberley a full week and still felt a great sense of despair mixed with both anger and confusion at what had transpired with Elizabeth. Had this been a form of retribution she had used to draw him in with her smiles, twinkling eyes, and endearing conversation, only to give him the greatest set down by not coming to his home when she had accepted his invitation? While he did not consider Elizabeth one who would resort to such behaviour, he could not come up with any other explanation.

He had received a letter from his cousin Fitzwilliam, inquiring whether he was still planning to join him at Rosings in May. Military duties had prevented his cousin from being able to make their annual trip over Easter. The thought of going back to the place where Elizabeth had refused his offer of marriage unsettled him, and he was not certain he wanted to make the trip, especially now. He wrote back to Fitzwilliam, telling him he would think on it and inform him of his decision as the time drew nearer.

He had been riding frequently since arriving at Pemberley. Despite the grandeur of his home, he felt restless and troubled inside its walls. One thing that gave him any sense of pleasure was galloping across the meadows and through the woods on Chalice, his Arabian horse. But since returning, even that did nothing to alleviate his confusion, torment, and pain.

He had much business to discuss with his steward, Mr. Evans, but felt distracted during his meetings, which was unusual for him. He felt the petty complaints and concerns of some of his tenants were nothing compared to what he was experiencing. He would then chide himself for his lack of compassion. Their worries were just as real and bothersome to them as his were to him.

The only other thing that he looked forward to each day – albeit with little hope of there being what he wished for – was the mail that was brought to Pemberley. He wondered whether Elizabeth would ever choose to write to him explaining her absence. Anything would suffice. But no letter from her or her aunt and uncle had yet arrived.

Georgiana would be arriving soon, and he was determined to put all these feelings aside for her sake. He needed to greet her with a cheerful disposition, devoid of all melancholy, so she would not be concerned for him.

On this clear early morning, he walked out to the stables and was greeted by a stable hand.

"Good morning, Mr. Darcy. Shall I ready Chalice for you?"

Darcy gave a nod, but then suddenly shook his head. "No, not this morning. Saddle up Gwendolyn for me."

"Gwendolyn?" He seemed surprised, then respectfully added, "Yes, sir."

When the horse was readied, he mounted the brown mare and let her set her own pace down the path. She was a gentle horse that always enjoyed a leisurely stroll, which was very much what he was in the mood for today. The horse had been the one upon which Georgiana had learned to ride. He knew his sister would always be completely safe on her, as the mare was calm and dependable. The horse was much older now, so he knew she would never bolt or rear up unexpectedly.

He greatly appreciated the warming temperatures, after having that unexpected drop in temperature in London. He despised ice, and when the storm had struck, he wondered if he would be able to travel back to Pemberley. Fortunately, the ice had not reached Derbyshire, although it had been slightly affected by the cold. The flowers that had already begun to bloom when the cold had briefly enveloped Pemberley seemed to have recovered well.

If only he was as resilient!

He sat upon Gwendolyn and looked out over the lake at the trees, sky, and clouds which were mirrored in the still, crystal blue water. He shook the reins, and the mare moved slowly along. He had often thought of Elizabeth and him walking the grounds of Pemberley together. He could imagine himself releasing all the burdens of being Master of Pemberley as he shared his thoughts, concerns, hopes, and dreams with her. He let out a huff and continued around the lake.

At length, he brought the horse to a halt, where he could now see the reflection of Pemberley in the water.

The horse whinnied, and Darcy chuckled. "It is a beautiful view, is it not?" He patted the horse's neck. "I know you miss being ridden. It is too bad Georgiana is not often at Pemberley."

He looked out across the grounds, which were now dotted with patches of green as new life was springing forth after the cold, barren winter.

The trees that towered to the east filtered the rising sun, allowing intermittent beams of light to pierce through, painting a delightful picture.

He looked back down to the lake as a light breeze sent small ripples across the water, distorting the image of the manor's reflection. His brows lowered as he considered that his image of Elizabeth was also now distorted with questions and uncertainties about her behaviour. No matter how much he pondered this, he could not reconcile who he believed her to be with what she had done.

When the sun finally peeked above the trees, he gave a light kick to Gwendolyn's sides. She begrudgingly took a few quick steps but then slowed down. He debated taking her down the path into the woods, but then decided that since it had been a while since she had been ridden, he would return her to the stables.

She seemed to know she would be returning to the shelter of the stables and took a few more quick strides, only to slow down again.

Darcy could not help but smile. "You are much like me, Gwendolyn. Eager to leave those places that cause you discomfiture and get back to where all is safe and secure." He shook his head. He found it difficult being in crowds and public places where he had few acquaintances. It was something with which he had always struggled and had been interpreted by Elizabeth and many in her small neighbourhood as him being arrogant and proud.

He could not change who he was, but he had believed... and hoped... that having Elizabeth by his side would help him when he found himself in those situations.

He grimaced as thoughts of her began to torment him again.

He came near Pemberley and pulled back on the reins when he saw someone leaving. He assumed they were delivering mail and was about to give the horse a kick but stopped himself. Shaking his head, he decided he would not hurry back just to see who had written to him. He was setting a new course, and it no longer involved Miss Elizabeth Bennet. He would allow Gwendolyn to take her own leisurely time back.

After handing Gwendolyn off to the stable hand, he returned to the house and purposely avoided his study, where the mail would have been taken. He bathed, changed, and sat down to read a book, but when it could no longer hold his interest, he walked to the study. There was only one piece of mail – a letter from Charles Bingley. He felt some disappointment that it had not been from Elizabeth but was delighted to hear from his friend. Darcy had not seen him since before Christmas. He tore the letter open and began to read.

Darcy ~ I regret that our paths have not crossed in quite some time. I have been up north, but I will be heading down to Hertfordshire in about a month. I need to decide what I should do with Netherfield. I can imagine what you are thinking about my actions, but I cannot seem to stop thinking of Miss Bennet. I still love her. I need to find out for myself whether her feelings for me were what I had believed them to be. I know what my feelings for her were, continue to be, and most likely always will be.

You always have an invitation to visit should you wish to join me, but please do not do so if your intent is to dissuade me of my affections for her. This is something I need to decide for myself.

Charles

Darcy's brows lowered. He knew that his friend's decision on what to do about Netherfield would hinge greatly on whether the eldest Miss Bennet still had feelings for him. He felt a gnawing regret deep inside for his actions that separated them. If it had not been for Bingley's sister prompting him to do so, instilling doubt in his own mind, would he have tried to dissuade him on his own? He knew part of his agreeing to collude with Miss Bingley was his desire to distance himself from Elizabeth. He dropped his hands to the table.

"What a mess the two of us have found ourselves in, and the blame rests solely on my shoulders!"

He bit his lower lip. A month would be enough time for him to complete the business he had with his steward and spend time with Georgiana when she arrived at Pemberley. He would likely enjoy a respite. But did he really want to step into that small village again knowing he would encounter Miss Elizabeth? Did he really want to hear what her reasons were for not visiting and offering no excuse, no apology? Did he really want to know what her true feelings for him were? His fingers nervously tapped the desk. She had once made her true feelings painfully clear to him.

He had time to dwell on this. He would concentrate on entertaining Georgiana, and when he felt the time was right, he would make his decision to either go visit Charles at Netherfield or to turn his back forever on Miss Elizabeth Bennet.

Chapter 6

Elizabeth was grateful to finally be back at Longbourn, in her own room and in her own bed. Despite needing some assistance moving about the house, and especially up the stairs to her room, she enjoyed being home. She had been gone far too long.

Her father had welcomed her home jubilantly. He had missed his favourite daughter, but his tender sentiments for her return quickly turned to teasing her for whatever it was that had distracted her, leading to the unfortunate accident. He accused her of becoming as silly as her sisters.

At length, however, she found herself being ignored by the others, as her two youngest sisters frequently had some extraordinary dilemma with which they were dealing. They often entangled their mother in it, and Mrs. Bennet was always willing to commiserate with Kitty and Lydia over some real or perceived plight, very often of some romantic sort. Their most recent quandary involved the two youngest sisters vying for the affections of the young and handsome Mr. Arnold, who was in Meryton visiting his aunt and uncle.

His arrival in the small town had prompted much speculation and excitement, especially amongst the single young ladies. He had attended the most recent assembly and had been declared to be an excellent dancer, an adept conversationalist, and a most amiable gentleman.

His aunt and uncle, who owned a small estate just outside of Meryton, had no children of their own and took great delight in introducing their nephew to the neighbourhood.

The neglect Elizabeth was now experiencing from most of her family was a relief to her, for she felt her aunt and uncle had been overly concerned for her well-being and spent more time with her than she would have wished. She loved them dearly but felt uneasy that she took their time away from their children and other obligations. Now that she was home, she enjoyed spending time with Jane, who did not coddle her, but also did not pity her. She felt her sister truly knew how she wished to be treated.

She was sitting in the parlour one afternoon when Jane came in after returning from a visit to the Lucases with their mother. Her face was pale, and her eyes wide. She tried to smile, but Elizabeth could readily see her distress.

"Jane, what is it?"

Jane settled down in the chair next to her and began knitting her fingers together. "Mrs. Lucas had some news. I do not know how I feel about it."

"And what is the news?"

Jane drew in a breath and cast her eyes down. "It appears that Mr. Bingley is returning to Netherfield." She looked up. "The house is being readied for him, not another tenant. He will soon be back in the neighbourhood!"

Elizabeth smiled. "Oh, Jane, I would argue that you *do* know how you feel about it. You are filled with the greatest hope that he is returning to see you again, this time to declare his love and admiration for you."

Jane shook her head. "I wish I could be certain of that, Lizzy. It has been well over a year since we have seen each other. That is not a strong indication of a fervent, constant love."

Elizabeth took her sister's hand, recollecting the words Mr. Darcy had spoken to her, rejoicing in his success in separating his friend from her sister. She shuddered at the very thought.

"I am certain he had his reasons for being away so long, but it is a good sign that he is finally returning."

Jane let out a soft sigh. "I imagine we shall soon find out, one way or another."

Elizabeth squeezed Jane's hand. "I will be here for you whether Mr. Bingley renews his affections or not. Just as you have been a support to me since my accident, I will be strong for you. You can count on me."

Jane wrapped her arms about her. "Thank you, Lizzy. I do not know what I would do without you."

When Jane left, Elizabeth was even more grateful she was home. She wondered whether Mr. Bingley was still influenced by Mr. Darcy and his caution to him regarding his affection for her sister. She let out a long sigh and slapped her hands on the arms of the chair.

"Oh, Mr. Bingley, I do hope you have chosen to make your own decision in the matter of love and not listen to anyone else!"

~~*

When Georgiana arrived at Pemberley, she took great delight in riding and walking around the property on pleasant days with her brother and playing the pianoforte during inclement weather. As they were both avid readers, they also spent a great amount of time in the library reading. She was only able to stay at their country home for a month due to a promise she had made to a friend to assist her in practicing the pianoforte, so Darcy wanted to make the most of the time she was there.

The month passed quickly, and Darcy often found her gazing at him, as if trying to determine whether he was still preoccupied with something – or someone. She had always been proficient at discerning his various moods, and he was certain she detected his lingering melancholy. She likely wished that he would openly speak to her about it. He had no desire to do so and was grateful she did not bring it up.

On the day before she and Mrs. Annesley were to return to London, she and her brother were in the library. Darcy was walking around searching the shelves for something, and Georgiana was seated reading a book.

"This is absurd!" he muttered, startling Georgiana so much she jumped.

"What is it, Fitzwilliam? Is something wrong?"

He turned and saw Georgiana sitting on the edge of her chair, leaning forward with a startled look on her face. He had completely forgotten she was there.

"No... nothing is wrong. I was just... I am trying to find a book, and it is not where it should be."

She gave him an encouraging smile. "I am certain you will eventually find it."

He gave a shrug and walked back to his chair, dropping into it.

"My belongings are being packed for my departure tomorrow." She inclined her head. "Do you know when you will be returning to London?"

Darcy's mouth twisted as he pondered this. "I am uncertain. It depends..."

When he said no more, she pursed her lips. Finally, she asked, "It depends... upon what?"

Darcy clasped his hands in his lap and looked down. "I... Georgiana, I have not mentioned this, but Bingley wrote to me before you arrived and informed me that he planned to return to Netherfield." He paused and drew up straight in the chair. After a moment, he said, "I will be joining him there shortly."

Her brows rose. "To Netherfield? In Hertfordshire?"

He silently nodded.

"I see. So, you are hoping to see Miss Bennet?"

Darcy's mouth grew dry, and he swallowed hard. "In all likelihood I shall."

"How long have you known you were going to do this?"

He began tapping his fingertips on the edge of his chair. "I have been contemplating whether or not to do this since I received the letter."

She chuckled and shook her head. "And you are just now informing me of this?"

He smiled at her. "I was unsure how to tell you. I did not think you would approve."

"And how often do you seek my approval before you do something?" She feigned a look of disgust. "You did not tell me you were going to ask for Miss Bennet's hand in marriage, let alone ask for my opinion on the matter."

He crossed his arms and leaned forward. "And what would you have said if I had written to you, asking for your opinion."

"Well, to own the truth, Brother, I often imagined that you would introduce me to the lady who would one day be my sister, before you asked her."

Darcy cradled his jaw with his hand. "I regret I did not do

that." He let out a long sigh. "As it was, I had no opportunity to do so." He leaned forward in the chair. "I often felt you would enjoy Miss Bennet's company, and she would enjoy yours. I believe the two of you would have liked each other very much. I hoped you both would."

Georgiana stood up and walked over to him, reaching out and taking his hand. "I know that any woman you choose to spend your life with will be someone I would grow to love."

"That means a great deal to me."

It was a moment before Darcy continued. "Bingley has likely already arrived in Hertfordshire."

"I see." She paused and drew in a breath. Very softly she asked, "Do you think it is wise for you to go? Perhaps it is time to let Miss Bennet go and find someone else."

Darcy dropped his head. "It is easier said than done." He looked up. "Do you remember when the litter of puppies were born in the stables, and Father told you that you could choose one of the puppies for a pet?"

A smile appeared on Georgiana's face. "Yes, but are you comparing Miss Bennet to a puppy?"

He laughed. "No, but it was how determined you were to choose one particular puppy. Each time we checked on the puppies as they were getting older, you went back to the same one. You would not consider any of the others."

"There was something special about Poppy." She let out a sigh. "I still miss her."

Darcy smiled. "You felt in your heart... all along... that she was the one for you."

Georgiana chuckled. "Unfortunately, Brother, there is one part of your story that does not correspond at all to your current situation."

"And what is that?"

"I took a liking to Poppy, and she took a very strong liking to me."

Darcy shrugged and looked away. "Well, be that as it may, as for your question on when I shall return to London, I cannot answer that, but..." He gave a slight shrug of his shoulders and turned back. "It all depends on what does – or does not – happen in Hertfordshire."

Her brows knit together. "I see."

"I can tell by your expression you are not of the opinion I should go." He rubbed his jaw. "I hardly know myself whether I ought to go, but... it is something I feel compelled to do."

"If it is something you feel you must do, then you must go."

Darcy gave her hand a squeeze and stood up. "Thank you for being so understanding and patient with me. You have helped me through this past month more than you know."

Georgiana stood up on her toes and kissed him on the cheek. "And you have always helped me more than you could ever know."

~~*

The next day, Darcy stepped out as the carriage was being loaded with Georgiana's and Mrs. Annesley's belongings. The two ladies soon came out, as well as Cook, who brought a basket full of food for them to eat on the long journey.

Georgiana came up to him. "I have enjoyed my time here with you, Brother."

"As have I with you, Georgiana. You know I always do."

"When will you leave for Hertfordshire?"

Darcy gave a quick shrug. "I have some business to tend to here that will likely take about a week. I hope to leave soon after."

Georgiana reached out and took his hand. "Please keep me advised on how you are doing. And let me know if there is anything I can do."

"Thank you, Georgiana. I will." He drew her close in an embrace. "Thank you for understanding. You will take care in London?"

"Yes, Brother, I will. And please, *you* take care of *yourself*... and your *heart* in Hertfordshire."

He gave her a half-hearted smile. "I will certainly try!"

Chapter 7

Elizabeth stood up from her chair and gingerly walked to the window, wincing in pain with each step. She gazed out and sighed. She had always loved this time of the year, when the grounds were bursting with colours from budding flowers, trees were laden with green leaves and blossoms, and white puffy clouds were moving lazily across the deep blue sky. She smiled and closed her eyes as the gentle rays of the sun infused her body with warmth.

Birds chirped excitedly, seeming to beckon her to step out and enjoy the day.

Her lips pressed together, and she dropped her head. How she wished she could go walking up Oakham Mount. The view the peak afforded would delight her eyes on a day such as today.

She wiggled her foot and gasped at the sharp pain, feeling a deepening surge of distress at her present circumstances. She took a few steps about the room, hoping – as she did daily – that the pain would eventually subside. But it did not seem inclined to do so.

Slowly walking back to the chair, she glanced down at her basket of needlework. She had always enjoyed passing the time using a needle and thread to stitch a sampler, decorate a pillow, or personalize the corner of a handkerchief, but she formerly relegated that work to cold and rainy days.

She sat down and picked up a linen handkerchief and searched through the colours of thread. She finally decided on shades of blue, green, and yellow to stitch some flowers. As she was threading the needle, Jane came into the room and sat down beside her.

"How are you feeling, Elizabeth?"

"I am well, although not as well as I would wish." She gestured towards the window. "Oakham Mount is beckoning me."

"I thought you might be feeling sorry for yourself on a day like today." Jane folded her hands, rubbing her thumbs together. "I would do anything for you if it meant you could get out and walk again, as you so love to do."

Elizabeth shrugged. "The physician says I might improve with time, so I have not given up all hope."

"I am glad."

"Did you and Mother have a pleasant visit with Aunt Phillips?" Elizabeth tilted her head. "Did she have any news... from the neighbourhood?"

Jane looked away and then back. "News?"

Elizabeth sent her a pointed look when she noticed a slight blush tint her sister's cheeks.

Jane let out a long sigh. "Yes, she did. Apparently Mr. Bingley has... he has returned to Netherfield."

Elizabeth reached over and took her sister's hand. "I am here for you, Jane. If you need a hug, need to talk, or... or if you need to cry on a shoulder, I am here for you."

Jane choked back a sob and squeezed Elizabeth's hand. "Thank you, dearest Lizzy." She tried to smile. "Have I told you how grateful I am that you are home?"

Elizabeth smiled. "Probably as many times as I have told you how glad I am to be here." She placed her other hand upon Jane's. "But however much you doubt me, I believe once Mr. Bingley sets his eyes on your pretty face again, sees your lovely smile, and observes your kindness and sweetness, he will no doubt profess his continuing, abiding love for you."

With a shrug, Jane said, "I cannot be so certain. I wonder if he will even call upon us. I doubt Father will pay him a call."

Elizabeth squeezed Jane's hand. "You know our Father. He will insist upon *not* visiting the man, but in the end, he shall do what is right." She bit her lip and silently thought to herself, *and hopefully Mr. Bingley will do what is right.*

She then wrapped her sister in a tight embrace.

~~*

One morning, a few days later, Elizabeth and Jane were in the parlour playing a duet on the pianoforte. They laughed when they played the wrong keys or got their fingers tangled together.

Behind them stood Mr. Arnold, the gentleman visiting his aunt and uncle in Meryton, and he was greatly enjoying their playing. Kitty and Lydia appeared to be enjoying it, as well, but Elizabeth was certain it was solely for the benefit of the esteemed young man, who had already visited Longbourn three times since arriving in the neighbourhood.

Mary sat upright in the corner quietly listening, eager for the opportunity to exhibit her skills on the pianoforte when her two elder sisters finished.

Elizabeth was certain Mr. Arnold had a fondness for Jane. She often found him gazing at her, engaging her in conversation, and frequently smiling in her direction. If her suspicions were correct, that might be just what Jane would need if Mr. Bingley did not renew his attentions. She chuckled as she thought it also could serve to propel Mr. Bingley to pursue Jane, as he might suffer from twinges of jealousy.

When they had finished playing, Mr. Arnold applauded. "Delightful, ladies! I enjoyed that immensely!"

Both ladies turned to face him and thanked him.

"You are too kind, Mr. Arnold," Jane said softly, prompting him to smile.

Elizabeth shook her head. "With such praise, I fear either you are not a student of music and did not notice our errors, or you are very well versed in music but are too polite, and therefore obligingly overlooked our mistakes and praised our efforts."

He chuckled. "You forgot one further possibility."

Elizabeth tilted her head. "And what might that be?"

"That I am both a student of music and – hopefully – polite, but in addition, I take great delight in the joy the performers exhibit while they are playing." He paused, looking at Jane and then back to Elizabeth. "You both had such expressions of merriment as you played. How could one not enjoy it?"

Elizabeth smiled. "That is indeed a noble trait to possess, for it allows one to overlook a lack of proficiency as long as the performer's joy is evident."

He gave an assenting nod. "Well, I must confess I am not an expert in music; however, I know enough about it to realize that it was a three-quarter measure piece." He crossed his arms and smiled.

"You are correct," Jane said.

"One to which you could waltz!" Lydia jumped up from her chair. "Have you learned the waltz, Mr. Arnold? How I would love to learn how to dance the waltz!" She began taking steps mimicking the dance.

Elizabeth sent her a warning glance. "Lydia, I do not think people in our neighbourhood would approve of the waltz."

With a scowl, Lydia said, "You only say that because you cannot dance!"

A look of disapproval crossed Kitty's face. "Lydia, that was not kind to say at all!"

"Well, I am certain Mr. Arnold has waltzed," Lydia insisted. "We all agreed after seeing you dance at the Meryton Assembly, that there was no finer dancer!"

"I thank you for your compliment, but I saw many that evening who were quite proficient at dancing. But as for the waltz, I own I have never danced it." Mr. Arnold shook his head. "In fact, I have yet to see it danced anywhere, although I know others who have."

Elizabeth shook her head at Lydia's forward manner towards the gentleman. At least it appeared she had forgotten about all the officers that had filled her mind the year before. She then looked apologetically at Mr. Arnold. "You must excuse our youngest sister, for she often gets some silly notions in her head that are not always easy to dispel."

Lydia propped her hands on her waist. "It is not a silly notion! If I want to dance the waltz, I will!" She let out a frustrated huff and then stormed out of the room.

Mr. Arnold gave a polite, somewhat awkward smile. "I believe there are mixed opinions about the waltz and whether or not it is proper."

"Pay no attention to Lydia, Mr. Arnold," Kitty said. "She has much to learn about life... and what is and is not proper."

Elizabeth smiled at Kitty's sudden display of maturity. Perhaps there was hope for her after all.

Mr. Arnold laughed. "Indeed, I remember myself at that age. Wanting to be an adult, or at least to be treated as an adult, but acting in ways that did not merit such treatment."

The gentleman and Bennet sisters continued to converse, and Mr. Arnold mentioned that he would be leaving for London in a few days.

"You are going to London?" Kitty asked.

"Yes, I must. I have some business there, but I shall return when it is completed."

"I am glad to hear that. We will miss your visits," Elizabeth said.

"Yes, Mr. Arnold, we most certainly will!" Kitty gave him a smile.

He acknowledged their compliment with a nod of his head. "Now, ladies, how about another duet?"

Jane and Elizabeth began looking through the pieces of music. Only Elizabeth noticed the look of disappointment cross Mary's face that she had not been given the opportunity to exhibit her piano skills. As the two sisters searched for a song to play, Hill stepped in to announce a visitor.

To the astonishment of the Bennet ladies, it was Mr Bingley!

Chapter 8

Elizabeth felt Jane's fingers wrap tightly about her wrist as they both fixed their eyes on the door.

Mr. Bingley stepped in with his familiar wide, congenial smile. His sparkling blue eyes quickly darted about the room, finally settling on Jane. He gave a quick bow. "I hope... I hope you do not mind my calling this morning unannounced." He began to rub his hands together. "I was out riding... it is such a beautiful day... and the next thing I knew, I was here."

Jane's breath hitched, but she said nothing.

Elizabeth readily noticed that despite his joviality, he seemed somewhat ill at ease. "It is a pleasure to see you again, Mr. Bingley. It has been far too long. Please, come in and have a seat." She stood up and gave Jane a nudge to do likewise as she extended her hand towards a chair.

"Yes, yes, please," Jane said in a whisper as she stood.

Elizabeth took Jane's arm, using it partially for support, but more so to encourage her sister to walk with her towards the gentleman. When Mary stood up to walk to the pianoforte, Elizabeth gave her head a quick shake and mouthed the words, "Not now."

Elizabeth turned to Mr. Bingley. "Have you become acquainted with Mr. Arnold? He is here visiting his aunt and uncle."

The two gentlemen faced each other, and Mr. Bingley's eyes widened. "Arnold? What are you doing here?"

"Are the two of you acquainted?" Elizabeth asked.

Mr. Arnold extended his hand. "As Miss Elizabeth said, I am visiting my aunt and uncle." He then turned to Elizabeth. "Yes, we are. We have a slight acquaintance through some mutual friends."

Turning back to Bingley, he asked, "And you? What brings you here?"

Mr. Bingley made a quick glance in Jane's direction, smiling as he did. "I lease a home nearby. Netherfield is about three miles from Longbourn."

"I did not know."

"Are you to stay long in the neighbourhood?" Bingley asked him.

"My plans are to remain until summer with an occasional trip back to London."

As the men continued to converse and acquaint each other on what had been happening in their lives, Elizabeth and Jane sat down. She noticed Mr. Bingley occasionally stealing nervous glances at Jane, and Mr. Arnold following his friend's gaze with apparent interest.

She discreetly lifted her foot and gently wriggled her ankle and toes to work through the pain from the simple walk across the room. She was grateful Mr. Bingley had not seemed to notice, engaged as he was in his conversation with Mr. Arnold and then turning his eyes only to Jane. If he had noticed her slight limp, he had been very polite and said nothing. Elizabeth was not averse to his finding out what had happened to her. She was certain that if he continued to see Jane, he would come to learn of her injury.

The men sat down, and they all began to converse. It was awkward at first, with occasional moments of silence and nervous glances about. Elizabeth did everything she could to encourage Jane to engage Mr. Bingley in conversation. Her sister appeared to be in shock at his sudden appearance, while he seemed apprehensive of the reason behind Jane's silence and reticent demeanour.

Elizabeth could not help but think of Mr. Darcy's excuse for separating Jane from Mr. Bingley, owing to his belief that she did not return the same depth of love for him that he had for her. If he were to see her now, she was certain he would feel justified in his misapprehension.

"Mr. Bingley," Elizabeth began. "Pray, what brings you back to Netherfield?"

He looked down at his hands, which he had tightly clasped. He looked back up and said, "Well, I had hoped to..."

Before he could finish answering, Mrs. Bennet burst into the room. "Why, Mr. Bingley! You have returned! How good it is to see you!" She pointed her finger at him. "We wondered what had become of you! You departed Netherfield without a word to anyone!" She cast her eyes in Jane's direction and then turned back to him as if expecting him to account for his long absence.

He gave a slight wince before his smile returned. "Yes, I do regret that. Things came up and I..." His voice trailed off. "I am deeply sorry."

Mrs. Bennet smiled. "Well, my good sir, we are not ones to find fault with anyone's actions. We are only glad you have finally returned!"

She walked over to the sideboard. "Where is the tea? Hill! Hill!" When the housekeeper stepped in, Mrs. Bennet pointed to the empty silver tray. "Please bring out some cake and more tea for our guests."

Hill nodded and picked up the tray and teapot. As she stepped out, Mr. Bennet came into the room.

"Good afternoon, Mr. Arnold and Mr. Bingley! What an occurrence for our household! Two gentlemen calling! I hope you are enjoying your visit."

"I can answer for myself," Mr. Arnold began. "I have enjoyed the company of your daughters very much. Your two eldest just performed a most delightful duet on the pianoforte."

"Good! I am glad to hear that!"

"You are too kind," Mrs. Bennet said. "And once Hill returns with the tea and cake, everything shall be perfect."

Mr. Bennet gratuitously smiled at his wife. "Yes, yes, Mrs. Bennet. But let us leave these young people alone, shall we?" He gently guided her to the door, and they walked out, with Mrs. Bennet's mumblings heard by those in the room.

Once they left, and Hill returned with refreshment, Jane thanked her and said she would take care of serving the others. She stood and asked if everyone would like some tea.

Mr. Bingley jumped to his feet and offered to assist her. Both Elizabeth and Mr. Arnold watched as the two stood at the sideboard and began conversing. Elizabeth smiled, but Mr. Arnold pinched his brows.

At length, he whispered to Elizabeth. "Is it my imagination or might there be something between the two of them?" He pressed his lips together as he awaited her answer.

Elizabeth smiled. "Is it that apparent to you?" Elizabeth noticed Mr. Arnold's brows crease. "Ah, I can see you are disappointed."

"Is it that apparent to *you*?" Arnold asked with a chuckle.

Elizabeth smiled. "I own that I noticed you seemed to favour her."

"But you say he has been gone a long time?"

She drew in a breath. "When he departed over a year ago, the two of them had grown very fond of each other. We were surprised when he did not return."

Mr. Arnold leaned back in his chair and folded his arms across his chest. "I am surprised. I would not consider that a smart thing for a gentleman to do – to leave a young lady as sweet and pretty as your sister without any word."

"He must have had his reasons," Elizabeth said. She gave a slight shrug of her shoulders. "Perhaps we will never know."

He looked at her and smiled. It was a warm, genuine smile, but she knew he was not likely to develop a fondness for her. They first met at the ball she attended when she had returned from London. She had declined his offer to dance and explained why. She had watched the enjoyment and proficiency he had exhibited while dancing and could agree with her younger sisters that he danced quite well.

It saddened her to think it was possible she would never dance again. Her steps were still too measured, her gait too wobbly, and her balance precarious.

She and Mr. Arnold talked for a short while, and as much as Elizabeth enjoyed his intelligence and humour, and even acknowledged he was certainly a handsome gentleman, she determined that she would encourage Kitty to join in the conversation. Despite her younger sister's youthfulness, she needed to learn the fine art of conversation. Kitty had matured greatly since the previous summer, but had always followed Lydia, who had the tendency to say whatever came to her mind. Kitty rode on the tails of those conversations, but never truly learned the art of carrying on a conversation herself.

She was not certain that Mr. Arnold had any interest in Kitty, but Elizabeth reasoned presently, that was probably for the best.

She smiled. She could certainly use Mr. Arnold to teach Kitty the fine art of conversing with others, especially a young gentleman. She looked over at her younger sister. "Kitty, I would imagine Mr. Arnold would be interested in hearing your opinion about the Cowper poems you just read." She turned to Mr. Arnold. "Are you familiar with his poems?"

He smiled. "I most certainly am."

Kitty's face lit up. She stood up and walked over to a table by the window and picked up a book. She returned, thumbing through the pages.

"Do you have a favourite?" he asked.

"I have not read all of them, but so far my favourite is 'Epitaph of a Hare.'"

He laughed. "That is a humorous one."

As they began to discuss the poem, Kitty became more and more animated. Elizabeth softly excused herself, citing fatigue. She stood up, walked towards the door and past Jane and Mr. Bingley, who paid her no heed, as they were engaged in pleasant conversation. Not one piece of cake had been served, nor cup of tea poured.

She stepped into the doorway and turned back to look at the two couples. She smiled at the scene before her. She was certain that Mr. Bingley still had strong feelings for Jane by the expression of his face, and she was confident he would soon make her an offer.

While she was not as certain about Mr. Arnold's feelings for Kitty, or hers for him, she knew this was a step towards her younger sister growing into a fine young lady.

Chapter 9

Darcy had been unable to depart Pemberley as soon as he had hoped, as a problem with one of his tenants required his attention. When that was finally settled, he had hoped to ride Chalice to make up for lost time, sending the carriage separately, but inclement weather prevented that, as well.

He finally deemed it preferable to ride in the carriage so he would not arrive at Netherfield clothed in a layer of dust and dirt, or even worse, mud. It was a long distance to travel, and he resigned himself to the confines of his carriage, where he would be alone with his thoughts as he pondered what would await him when he arrived in Hertfordshire. Chalice went along, as well, tethered to the equipage.

For the past few days, his mind was engaged in the details of his tenant's issue, and he had not the time to dwell on his impending visit. But once he had a plan in place and that task had been completed, he felt a small knot deep within that had continued to grow. He shook his head as he stared out the window of his carriage, wondering why he was even doing this.

He fisted his hand and began to pound his chin. It was probably not the wisest thing he had ever done. He was not certain whether he wanted to give Elizabeth another chance to explain her absence or to make sure she knew that she had been at fault by not advising him of a change in their plans.

He dropped his head back and closed his eyes. He felt a mixture of anger, hope, desperation, dread, and anticipation. He let out a groan, wondering how this young lady had such power over his sensibilities. He made a vow that this would be his last attempt to learn the truth about that day, to give her another chance to account for her actions and to discover what her true feelings for him were.

A long day on the road was followed by a stay at an inn. An early start the next morning produced the same myriad thoughts and feelings as he drew nearer to Hertfordshire and the neighbourhood of Meryton.

At length, his carriage took the turn in the road that would take him to Netherfield. His head unwittingly turned in the opposite direction, towards Longbourn. The lurch in his stomach reminded him that he knew not whether he was ready to face Elizabeth again.

The carriage pulled up to his friend's modest but impressive estate and stopped. The door was opened, and he stepped out. He stretched out his legs and ran his hands over his garments, in a futile attempt to straighten out any wrinkles that had formed from the long ride.

As he took long strides towards the house, he wondered whether Bingley would be home. Would he be visiting Longbourn? Would Miss Bennet be visiting him here? Might Elizabeth even be here? He had to mentally prepare himself for every possibility.

When he stepped up to the door and lifted his hand to knock, he abruptly stopped. What if Miss Bingley was here, and her brother was not? She was the last person he wished to see, and he clenched his fists just at the thought. If it turned out she was at Netherfield, and Bingley at Longbourn, he would make the excuse that he needed to leave and see him at once.

He rapped on the door and waited; his heart pounded as a reminder to him of what might soon happen.

Brownwood opened the door and looked surprised to see Darcy standing there.

"Mr. Darcy, it is good to see you." He stepped aside to allow him entrance. "We were not informed you would be coming."

"I was not certain when I would arrive. If it is more convenient, I will make arrangements to stay at the inn in Meryton."

"Of course, it is not inconvenient. I will have your room readied at once."

"Is Bingley at home?"

"No, sir. He is at Longbourn."

Darcy drew in a hitched breath. "I... I will have my belongings brought in and will leave you to prepare my room, however..." He paused. "I will wait to have them unpacked until later. I am not certain I will be staying."

"As you wish, sir."

"Thank you. I shall set off for Longbourn directly."

"Yes, sir."

Darcy walked back to the carriage and instructed his valet to take his valises inside but to leave everything packed until he returned.

If his valet was surprised, he did not show it. A polite nod of the head assured Darcy that he would do as he bid.

As his belongings were unloaded, Darcy had Chalice saddled. He paced nervously about as he waited, kicking up the dirt with his boots. He then chided himself for covering himself with the same dirt he had hoped to avoid when he decided to ride in the carriage.

When Chalice was saddled, he quickly mounted the horse. He drew in a deep breath, hoping vainly to calm his heart, but it was to no avail. In a few minutes he would know all. And what he found out would either bring him reassurance of either her continued contempt or... more preferably... of those changed feelings that she had expressed to him in the bookstore.

He could not decide if he wanted to gallop the three miles to Longbourn or to proceed leisurely. The horse was certainly capable of doing either, but his heart was unable to do the latter. It was racing no matter the speed of the horse.

He finally decided to walk Chalice so he could think through what he might say when he saw Elizabeth. He certainly had not thought ahead when he had gone to ask for her hand. He had been rude, demeaning, and the only passion he had exhibited was in reinforcing to her how far beneath him she was and how her family displayed little decorum. He shuddered. He did not want a repeat of that debacle.

As he pondered the impending visit, he knew there would likely not be an opportunity to speak with her alone in her house. With four sisters and a meddlesome mother, an occasion might not present itself. He thought he might be able to tell by her expression and reaction to seeing him again how she felt, but he would prefer to hear her say it. He then got an idea that since it was such a pleasant day, an offer to walk might provide them the chance to speak alone.

At length, he could see Longbourn in the distance. He brought the horse to a stop and drew in a deep breath. He felt as winded as if he had walked the three miles himself. He let out a sigh as he recollected Elizabeth's brightened complexion after walking the same three miles to visit her ailing sister at Netherfield. It was that morning that a hopeless love for her had begun to take root in his heart.

Once at Longbourn, he dismounted and wrapped the reins about a post, swallowing hard in a vain attempt to alleviate the discomfort of his dry throat and mouth. He was now only moments away from facing Elizabeth Bennet again, the first time since seeing her in the bookstore.

He rubbed his hands together as he walked up to the door. He knocked briskly and stepped back. The door was answered quickly, and he inquired whether the family was at home.

The portly housekeeper nodded and said several were in the parlour. "Your friend, Mr. Bingley is here, as well."

He followed her to the parlour, peering over her head into the room in anticipation of seeing Elizabeth's face. He heard her soft laugh first, and glanced around, finally setting his eyes on her.

She appeared to be conversing with someone he could not see as Bingley was blocking his view. He straightened up in nervous anticipation and kept his eyes on Elizabeth's face as Hill announced him and stepped aside to allow him to enter.

He readily noticed the astonished look on Elizabeth's face when she turned her head. The smile that had been on her face quickly disappeared. Her brows lowered, and she seemed to draw back. He could not observe much more, for Bingley stood up quickly and walked over to him, extending his hand. As he grasped his friend's hand in a greeting, he noticed another gentleman seated beside Elizabeth. He did not look familiar; he did not remember seeing him when he was last in the neighbourhood.

"Darcy!" Bingley exclaimed. "What brings you here? I had no

idea you were coming."

"I... It was a last-minute decision. I was on my way to London and thought I would stop by to see you. I hope you do not mind."

"Of course not. I assume you received my letter about returning to Netherfield."

"I did."

Darcy noticed a brief look of concern on his friend's face, possibly a result of believing he had come to try to separate him again from Miss Bennet. He gave him a reassuring smile that he hoped would alleviate any fears he might have in that field.

When he stepped in and walked towards the others, he studied Elizabeth. She sat with a small coverlet over her lap, and her eyes looked everywhere but at him.

"Darcy, are you acquainted with Jacob Arnold?" Bingley asked.

He looked at the man who had been seated between Elizabeth and one of her sisters. He could not recollect her name.

"No, I do not believe we are acquainted."

The gentleman stood up, and Bingley made the introductions.

Once they had been introduced, Jane extended her hand towards a chair. "Would you care to sit down, Mr. Darcy?"

He doubted whether he would be able to relax in a chair, but he muttered a thank you and walked over to sit down. He was seated across from Elizabeth, who still seemed unable – or unwilling – to meet his eyes.

Conversation continued amongst the small party of people. He could not tend to the conversation, as he debated whether to come out and ask Elizabeth what had prevented her from coming to his home after she had accepted his invitation.

His eyes turned to Arnold, and he decided not to bring it up. He had no idea if she had even mentioned their encounter and the invitation to anyone, and he wished not to make her uneasy. He needed to speak with her privately.

He abruptly stood up and walked to the window to look out, waiting for the right moment to suggest a walk outdoors. At that moment, Mrs. Bennet came into the room.

He felt his entire body tense from head to toe when she called out, "Mr. Darcy! I had not been informed that you were here." She walked over to the sideboard and looked over the refreshment that had been put out. She picked up a small piece of cake and turned back around.

"I hope you do not mind, Mrs. Bennet."

She waved her hand through the air. "Of course not! After all, my Lizzy visited your home in Derbyshire last summer and claimed it to be one of the most beautiful homes she has ever seen!"

Darcy started. "Pardon me?"

"Yes," she said as she took a small bite. "Lizzy walked through Pemberley last summer with her aunt and uncle."

Darcy spun his head around to look at Elizabeth.

"Mother!" Elizabeth's face had grown pale, and a look of distress crossed her features.

Darcy could not speak. If Elizabeth had been to his home, why had she not mentioned that to him in the bookstore? He turned to Elizabeth. "You visited Pemberley?"

He watched her draw in a long breath. "Yes. My aunt grew up in Lambton, and we were visiting there, and they suggested we go see it." She let out a nervous laugh. "I did not feel that we should, but my aunt insisted." She cast her eyes towards her mother and then back to him. "We understood you were from home, and so we decided there would be no harm in taking a tour of it."

"Oh, I am certain Mr. Darcy would have been delighted to see you if he had been home!" Mrs. Bennet looked at the gentleman.

"Yes... yes, it would have been a pleasure to see you." Obviously, Elizabeth had not informed her mother of his proposal – and her rejection of it. He believed he knew why. But what did this mean? Did this have any bearing on why she may have changed her mind to visit him?

Darcy turned in frustration back to the window and then spun around, looking directly at Elizabeth. "As it is such a pleasant day, might I suggest a walk outdoors?"

Bingley jumped up. "That is a splendid idea!" He looked at Jane. "Miss Bennet, would you care to walk?"

She smiled. "I would."

Darcy watched Elizabeth reach out to smooth the coverlet on her lap. He noticed her wince, and she shook her head. "I think not, thank you." She clasped her hands tightly together and turned to Kitty and Mr. Arnold. "You are free to join them."

Mr. Arnold spoke. "It is a fine idea, Darcy, but I need to take my leave soon."

"I do not wish to, either," Kitty said.

"It seems it will be just the three of you." Arnold leaned back into his chair, appearing to Darcy as if he were not planning to leave any time soon.

He clenched his fist, knowing precisely what this meant. He gathered from the scene unfolding in front of him that Elizabeth had no interest in defending her actions – or inaction – that day in London, and he could now guess why. Mr. Arnold!

He gave a quick bow. "It was a pleasure seeing you again." Turning to Bingley, he said, "I shall be outside."

"Let me retrieve my shawl," Jane said.

Bingley came to Darcy's side. "Come, I will wait outside with you."

When the two men stepped out, Bingley propped his arms on his waist. "I want you to know, Darcy, that I am as much in love with Miss Bennet as I was when I last left Netherfield, and I am firmly convinced she feels the same. You might as well dismiss any effort on your part to dissuade me of an attachment."

Darcy attempted to smile, as difficult as he found it to be. "I have no intention of doing that."

"Oh? Good, I am glad to hear that!"

"Does she know your true feelings?"

Bingley shook his head. "I have not had a single opportunity to confess them to her, as someone is always with us."

Darcy pressed his lips together in thought. "Bingley, as no one else will be joining us on this walk, I shall return to Netherfield and allow you all the time you need alone with Miss Bennet to express your true sentiments."

"Would you do that?"

"I would." He paused. "Please convey my regrets to her that I was unable to join you."

"I will! I shall!"

Darcy extended his hand, clasping his friend's in a firm grip. He walked to his horse and mounted. Before pulling the reins to direct it away, he looked back. "Bingley, I do sincerely wish you and Miss Bennet great joy!" He then kicked the horse, taking him away from Longbourn and Miss Elizabeth Bennet forever.

Chapter 10

Elizabeth sat on her bed waiting for Jane to return from her walk with Mr. Bingley and Mr. Darcy. Earlier she had been so astonished by the latter's visit that she felt she could no longer enjoy any conversation, including Mr. Arnold's attempts to engage her. She had gone upstairs to her room shortly after Jane stepped out to join the two gentlemen.

She hoped by taking her leave of the small party in the parlour that it might give Kitty another opportunity to converse with Mr. Arnold and possibly win him over. It appeared that he was still paying more attention to herself than her younger sister, although she could not imagine why.

She looked down at her foot, wondering if she would ever walk again without a limp. Would she be able to step out on a ballroom floor and dance without stumbling? Would she be able to take a gentleman's arm and not have to use it for support? Would she be able to take a stroll outside again as she so wished she could have done today?

Her brows pinched in thought. Why had Mr. Darcy asked if anyone wished to take a walk? He knew she enjoyed walking. She doubted he knew of her injury and would have assumed she would join him. He had directed his gaze upon her when he suggested it. She could not forget the way he had stared at her most of the time he was there.

"Why did he even come?" She pounded her fist on the pillow.

She wondered whether Jane mentioned her accident and her present condition to him as they walked. If she had, Elizabeth deemed it likely that he was now congratulating himself on not being tied to a woman who was imperfect, crippled, and who would not be able to accompany him to all the high society events in London without being looked upon with disdain.

As tears began to fill her eyes, she took in several hitched breaths. She had never regretted her decision to refuse his proposal, even after learning more about his good character and how greatly she had misjudged him. The explanations he had put forth in his letter to her had begun that transformation, and what she learned about him from his housekeeper at Pemberley had done even more to convince her of her error. For some reason, however, she was now feeling a deep sense of regret that she could not account for. There was something that eluded her.

"Oh!" she fell back onto the bed.

There was a knock at the door, and she sat back up, quickly dabbing her eyes with her handkerchief. "Come in."

Jane walked in, her face beaming. She stretched her arms towards her sister.

"Oh, Lizzy! I am so happy! Mr. Bingley told me how much he still loves me – he has always loved me and never stopped – and he asked me to marry him!"

Elizabeth drew her sister into a hug. "Jane, I am so happy for you! That is wonderful news!"

Jane's smile was infectious. "He is now speaking with Father." She grew pensive. "Ever since he came back into the neighbourhood, I have tried not to hold on to the hope that he felt the same."

"But he does. Jane, I knew he did. I could readily see it."

"Could you?"

Elizabeth nodded. "Even Mr. Arnold noticed it." She tilted her head. "And pray what did Mr. Darcy have to say about this?"

Jane's brows pinched. "Mr. Darcy?"

Elizabeth chuckled. "He did accompany you on your walk, did he not? Did he keep ten paces behind you to allow you time to talk to Mr. Bingley alone?"

"Oh," Jane said softly. "I never once thought of him. He was gone when I stepped out."

"Gone?"

Jane shrugged. "I suppose he returned to Netherfield. He did not join us."

"Perhaps that was his design in coming, then, to suggest a walk, giving Mr. Bingley an opportunity to spend some time alone with you."

"Lizzy, do you think he would have done that?"

Despite offering this possibility to her sister, she thought it more likely that when the two men stepped out together, he had made one last attempt to talk Mr. Bingley out of an attachment. When he failed, he had left.

"I have no idea." She pursed her lips. "But in truth, I cannot account for his coming to Longbourn at all today. The last time he and I saw each other at Kent, it was most unpleasant. I know he must despise me, and he had to know he would see me."

Jane took her hand and squeezed it. "Perhaps he holds no resentment, and he was merely eager to see Mr. Bingley."

"And put both himself and me in such an awkward situation?" She gave a shrug. "No, Jane. I could see in the way he looked at me that he was still angry with me. He glared at me as if he were waiting for me to say something to him, to apologize for the words I spoke to him a year ago, for the opinion I had of him."

Jane shook her head. "Oh, I am certain he was doing no such thing."

"But I could clearly see the shocked look on his face when Mother told him I had been to Pemberley. Oh, I wish she had not mentioned it!"

"But why, Lizzy? Many people tour places like that. There is nothing wrong with it."

Elizabeth shook her head. "It is perfectly acceptable, except when the person is touring the home of the man who asked for her hand and whom she turned down in a most insulting manner." She let out a sigh. "I cannot imagine what he is thinking of me now."

"He has likely completely forgotten about it."

"Perhaps, although I strongly doubt it." She gestured towards the door. "Now you should go prepare Mother for the news. Try to help her remain calm and to keep her boisterous celebration as quiet as possible."

"Yes, I will try to do that, but please consider this, Lizzy. With my engagement to Mr. Bingley, you will likely be much in Mr.

Darcy's company." She bit her lip and said, "Of course, I would like you to be my bridesmaid..."

"Oh, Jane, I would love to!"

Jane took in a breath. "And Charles is going to ask Mr. Darcy to stand up for him."

"I see."

"Please try to be civil to him when you see him and not expect the worst of what his thoughts, feelings, or motives might be."

Elizabeth gave her sister's hand a squeeze. "For your sake and happiness, I think I can do all those things, even if he cannot."

She watched Jane leave the room, and she put her hand over her heart. If she felt Mr. Darcy had come only to find more fault with her, why was she feeling this inexplicable tenderness towards him? From where did it come?

She pounded her fist on her pillow again. "Oh! I do not know what to think about him!"

~~*

Darcy arrived at his home in London just as the sun was just setting. He was glad to be home and away from Hertfordshire, Longbourn, and Miss Elizabeth Bennet.

He was grateful for two things: first, that he had tethered Chalice to the carriage as they travelled from Pemberley to Netherfield, which allowed him to ride the horse back to London, and secondly, that he had told his valet not to unpack his trunk. After departing Longbourn and informing his valet that he would not be remaining, he chose to leave directly for London. He told his valet he could either spend the night at Netherfield and leave in the morning or leave directly and spend the night on the road at an inn.

He dismounted the horse and fisted his hands. The reception he had received from Elizabeth was enough to convince him of her indifference; her dislike and disdain of him remained. "She is now lost to me forever!" The lurch in his heart made him doubt that he would ever be free of her, but he would make every attempt.

It had been good for his spirits to ride Chalice away from

Longbourn and Elizabeth Bennet. He had pushed the horse as hard on the road as he tried to push Elizabeth from his thoughts. But removing her from his heart would be more difficult.

While he had been riding to London, he determined he would throw himself into London society, as contemptible as much of it was to him, and keep himself busy and occupied with all things completely unrelated to her!

He stepped into his house and was greeted by the footman and his housekeeper. He asked that a bath be drawn before sitting down to dine. He went to Georgiana's room and rapped lightly at the door.

She bid him enter, and her eyes widened when she saw him. "Fitzwilliam! You are home!" She rushed over to him, and he wrapped her tightly in his arms.

"Yes, I am."

She drew back and studied his face. "You have a smile on your face, but I can see that you are distressed. Did it not go well in Hertfordshire?"

Darcy drew in a deep breath. "It was apparent to me that Miss Bennet did not wish to speak to me. She offered no explanation and seemed engaged in the company of another young man who was there. I realized there must not have been any substance to the hopes that I have recently clung to so foolishly."

"I am so sorry," she said. "I had hoped..."

"Yes, as had I, but those hopes were all in vain." He gave her a resigned smile. "I would prefer not to discuss it now. Have you eaten?"

Georgiana nodded.

"I assumed so. I have not, but I need to freshen up first, and then I shall go down to eat in about an hour." He leaned over and kissed the top of her head. "If you would like to join me, I will tell you all about it then."

Chapter 11

When Darcy came down to dine, Georgiana was already there, waiting for him. She was taking small bites of a lemon scone. When he saw her, a small smile appeared on her loving face.

"Either you are very eager to hear all the disheartening details of my encounter with Miss Bennet, or you discovered you were still hungry."

She lifted the scone up towards him. "You know I cannot resist a lemon scone." She took another bite. "It gives me no pleasure to hear of your distress, Brother. I only wish to provide you with encouragement, if you need it, and reassurances that you are still good and honourable, since you most likely *will* need that."

He sent her a questioning glance.

"I imagine the words she spoke to you when she turned down your suit are still churning about inside your head, and with her offering you no explanation for why she did not visit you in London, you assume she still feels the same way."

"That was almost a year ago, now."

Georgiana took another bite of the scone. When she had finished it, she said very softly, "The woman that you love and admire thinks poorly of you. I imagine that has you questioning everything about yourself."

Darcy chuckled. "When did you become such an expert on human nature?"

She gave a shrug. "I am not at all an expert on human nature, but perhaps, Fitzwilliam, I am an expert on your nature." She folded her hands in her lap. "Now, would you please tell me all that happened in Hertfordshire?"

"I am still not certain I want to talk about it. Besides, there is not much to tell."

She smiled. "Then we shall not be here long." She paused and waited for him to begin.

Darcy's short tale of woe took about twenty minutes to relate to his sister, with her occasionally asking him a question. When he had finished, she looked at him sadly.

"I am deeply sorry you were not able to speak with her alone. Perhaps, however, if Miss Jane Bennet accepts Mr. Bingley's offer of marriage, you will have another opportunity to speak with her at the wedding."

Darcy's face darkened, and he took a moment before answering. "I... I do not think..." He began to rub his jaw. "I will likely not be attending his wedding."

Georgiana's eyes widened. "Fitzwilliam! He is your good friend!" She shook her head. "No, he is more than that. He is your closest friend! How can you not attend his wedding?"

Darcy felt his stomach begin to churn. "Just the thought..." He drew himself erect. "Besides, I feel I must go to Rosings."

Georgiana shook her head. "Do you truly find a visit with our aunt preferable to another encounter with Miss Bennet?"

He let out a slow breath. "No, but I have learned to dismiss our aunt's proclivities for the absurd and can walk away from them without any injury to myself." He looked away. "But I cannot say the same about Miss Elizabeth."

Georgiana let out a soft sigh and stood. She walked over to her brother and placed her hand on his shoulder. "I am so sorry things did not work out as you wished." She leaned over and kissed his cheek. "I shall ready myself for bed. Goodnight, dearest Brother."

Darcy reached up and grabbed her hand, giving it a squeeze. "Goodnight, Georgiana. You are a dear treasure to me."

"As you are to me."

When she left the room, Darcy looked down at his plate. He had only taken a few bites of his meal but was not in the least bit hungry. He pushed himself away from the table and stood up.

"Miss Elizabeth Bennet, I now vow to put all thoughts of you out of my head and push all feelings for you out of my heart." He gave a shudder, and he realized with a gripping pain that it would be more difficult than he ever imagined.

Elizabeth was almost grateful for her injury, for it gave her the opportunity to take refuge in her room when her mother's nerves were at their most explosive. Planning a wedding, while the most blessed thing in her mind to do, was also the most stressful.

Having the dresses made, planning the meal, and arranging all the other details had been taking a toll on her and everyone else in the Bennet household in the weeks since Jane and Mr. Bingley's engagement.

While she was resting in her room one afternoon, a week before the wedding, Jane tapped on Elizabeth's door.

"Come in," Elizabeth said.

When Jane stepped in, Elizabeth shook her head. "You know you do not need to knock."

"I did not wish to waken you if you were asleep."

"Jane, I am no longer suffering fatigue from my injuries." She slumped her shoulders and let out a soft moan as she heard a wail of vexation from her mother. "I merely wish for a little peace and quiet."

Jane sat down on the bed next to Elizabeth. "Mr. Arnold came by earlier and asked for you."

Elizabeth dropped her head. "I cannot imagine why he is seeking me out. I have done everything I can to encourage his attentions towards Kitty."

"I wonder if he views Kitty as too young."

"Yes, she is young, and I do not feel as though she is at all ready to marry, but I am convinced conversing with him is good for her." She gave a shrug. "Besides, we are not the only eligible young ladies in the neighbourhood." She let out a huff. "And none are in a broken state as I am."

"Lizzy, you are not broken!"

"I am certainly not whole. I limp, I am in pain when I walk, and I will likely never dance again." She shrugged her shoulders. "The man loves to dance, is an extremely proficient dancer, and I would never be able to stand up to dance with him."

Jane took her hand. "You do not know that." She tilted her

71

head. "Do you feel as though there has been any improvement?"

Elizabeth shrugged her shoulders. "It is hard to tell. If there has been improvement, it is happening so slowly that I am not certain. There are times I think it is getting better, but the next moment I wonder if it is just my imagination."

"I am certain there must have been a little improvement." Jane gave her an encouraging smile.

"Tell me, did Mr. Arnold stay long? Did he have the opportunity to speak with Kitty at all?"

"With Mother, Lydia, and Mary also in the parlour with him, it made it a little difficult." Jane pinched her brows. "Kitty does not seem to converse well when Lydia is with her."

Elizabeth chuckled. "It is likely because Lydia does most of the talking. Kitty has never been assertive in that way."

Jane shook her head. "Between Mother and Lydia, Kitty could not have gotten a word in even if she tried."

"Poor Kitty. I do believe she likes him. I am grateful Lydia no longer thinks him suitable for her." She chuckled. "I believe she learned early on that he did not respond to her flirting."

Jane smiled. "Mr. Bingley also came by."

"Did he? And what did he have to say?" She leaned in. "Have his sisters come to Netherfield yet? Are they eager to welcome you into their family with open arms?"

"No, they have not yet arrived. I think they are due a few days before the wedding."

"I see."

"But Lizzy, there is something that does have him somewhat distressed."

"What is that?"

"He has heard from Mr. Darcy, and he told him that he will not be able to attend the wedding."

Elizabeth felt an inexplicable disappointment, that must have been reflected on her face.

Jane squeezed her hand. "What is it, Lizzy? You seem somewhat distressed."

Elizabeth put her hands up to her face. "Do I?" She tried to smile. "I do not know what it is, Jane, but I..." She paused and drew in a breath. "I cannot account for it, but ever since Mr.

Darcy came that afternoon, I have..." She dropped her hands in her lap and looked down.

Jane leaned in. "You have what?"

"I have had these fleeting thoughts and feelings about him... *for* him." She looked up and shook her head. "When you told me just now that he is not coming to the wedding, I felt a pang of sadness, of disappointment that I would not see him."

"Well, you did say after touring Pemberley and hearing the admiration his housekeeper had for him that you had begun to see him in a better light."

Elizabeth pinched her brows. "Yes, but this is different. It is as if there is something I cannot fully recollect. Something teasing my thoughts." She squeezed Jane's hand. "As I said, I cannot account for it. Perhaps I am just feeling sorry for myself and my injuries, and if I had accepted his proposal, I would be walking without any trouble through his beautiful home and grounds of Pemberley." She gave a shrug. "Did Mr. Bingley say why Mr. Darcy was not coming? I always felt they were the best of friends." If Elizabeth were to guess, she was certain it was because Mr. Darcy still did not approve of his friend marrying her sister.

"I believe he said he had to visit his aunt at Rosings."

"Oh, yes. I understand he visits her every spring." Elizabeth wondered what memories he would be taking with him as he went. Would he be plagued with the uncaring way she had refused his suit, the accusations she had hurled at him, and the way she had demeaned his character?

There was silence for a moment and then Jane smiled. "I understand your gown for the wedding is completed. Are you pleased with it?"

Elizabeth laughed. "Of course, I am, but are you pleased with *your* gown? That is more important."

"Yes. It is beautiful. There are just a few more things that need to be done." A smile appeared. "Oh, Lizzy! I am so happy. I do not deserve to be so happy!"

Elizabeth propped her hands on her waist. "On the contrary, Jane. You, of all people, deserve the greatest happiness!"

"I confess I am profoundly happy. I truly am."

"Jane, speaking of gowns, would you be able to get my teal

reticule out of the closet? I thought it would look nice with my dress. I think it will go nicely with the teal ribbons on it, but I want to see how well it matches."

"I would be more than happy to." Jane walked over to the closet and opened the door.

"Thank you. I have not had any need for it recently, but it should be tucked in a basket with the others."

Jane looked around and finally pulled it out. "Here it is, but there are some smudges of dirt on it. It needs to be cleaned."

Elizabeth reached out and took it from Jane's hand. "Oh, it certainly is soiled. I wonder..." She paused and then looked up. "I know I took this with me when I went to Aunt and Uncle Gardiner's. I wonder if I was carrying it when I fell."

"Perhaps you were."

Elizabeth turned it over in her hand, fingering the lace and corded handle. "This has always been my favourite reticule, and I think it will look perfect with my dress."

"I believe you are correct," Jane said. "I shall leave you now. I will be in my room for a while if you need anything."

"Thank you, dearest Jane."

When Jane stepped out, Elizabeth turned the reticule over in her hands. She fingered the lace, wincing at a few places where it had ripped.

She reached inside and felt a few items, pulling them out. She had a comb and pins, some coins, and a few pieces of paper. She glanced down at one, which appeared to be a list she had made of things she wanted to look at while at the clothing shop with her aunt and uncle. She gave her head a shake, as she did not remember writing it at all.

"I still cannot recollect anything from that day."

She gave a shrug and picked up a rather stiff piece of paper. A card of some sort with writing on it. She looked down at it and felt a wave of confusion overwhelm her.

Her fingers began to tremble as she looked down at the name printed on the card. It was the name and London address of Fitzwilliam Darcy. She squinted her eyes, as if she were reading it wrong.

She fingered the fine linen card and slowly turned it over,

wondering how it had ever ended up in her reticule and when she had received it.

She gasped when she saw the meticulous handwriting staring back at her. It said, *'Four O'Clock, Until then, Fitzwilliam Darcy.'*

Her mouth went dry as she was suddenly assaulted with a barrage of images of a bookstore, a conversation, a smile, a look, a laugh. She looked up in horror as shivers began to course through her as she recollected the invitation he extended to her and her aunt and uncle to visit him the following day at his home in London. Her chest constricted, and she could barely take in a breath.

"Jane! Jane!" she called out. "Jane, come here! Quickly!"

Chapter 12

Jane hurried to her sister's side. "What happened, Lizzy? What is wrong?"

Elizabeth lifted the reticule up in one hand and the card in the other, both hands shaking.

"I found this... I found this card in the reticule." Her voice increasingly trembled as she spoke.

"What is this?" Jane asked as she reached for the card. Her eyes widened as she read the side with the handwritten name and time. "What does this mean? Why do you have this?"

Elizabeth closed her eyes and dropped her head as she attempted to school her thoughts and emotions. "I remember, Jane. I remember everything." She opened her eyes and pointed down to the card. "This... this... Mr. Darcy gave it to me in the bookstore." She looked up and met Jane's questioning expression.

"Lizzy, I fear I do not understand."

"We met... Mr. Darcy and I met in the bookstore across the street from where our aunt and uncle were trying on their new clothes. We talked. It was all very friendly. He was very polite and amiable and invited us to his home the next day!" Tears began to pool in her eyes.

Jane's jaw dropped as she looked back at the card and turned it over and read the address. "You were invited to his home in Grosvenor Square." She then shook her head. "But why did he not say something when he came? Why did he not inquire how you were faring?"

"Oh, Jane! Do you not see? It is because he was not aware of my injury. He left the bookstore several minutes before I did." She let out a long sigh. "He must have assumed the worst about me when we did not come the next day without any sort of explanation or apology."

"Do you think he came to Longbourn to inquire why you did not come?"

Elizabeth gave a little shrug. "I cannot be certain, but I would assume so. That was why he kept looking at me. He wanted me to explain our absence that day." She grasped Jane's hand. "He must think me devoid of all decency."

"And then he left Netherfield before Charles returned from Longbourn, so he likely still does not know." Her eyes lit up. "I will ask Charles to write to him. To explain!"

Elizabeth smiled. "Jane, you have a wedding coming up. His family and guests will be arriving, and that will be the last thing he needs to worry about. It can wait until after the wedding."

"Are you certain?"

Elizabeth gave a shrug. "It matters not. In my condition, he will likely not desire to renew any of the affection he felt towards me, but..." She paused and drew in a breath. "I would hate to have him thinking the worst of me... of my lack of courtesy and manners."

"But certainly, if he took the time to come to Hertfordshire, and especially to Longbourn, he must still have feelings for you."

Elizabeth let out a sarcastic huff. "My condition is not something a gentleman of high standing would want to shackle himself with." Elizabeth felt her head spin, and she placed her hand on her forehead. "Oh, Jane. Now I know why I felt such tenderness towards him that day he came. He had been so kind... so forgiving... and after our encounter, I felt that I could never love anyone more than I loved him at that moment."

"Oh, Lizzy, do you truly feel this way?"

Elizabeth wiped away a tear and lifted her eyes to Jane. "Do you remember what Aunt Gardiner told us about knowing when we loved someone?"

Jane let out a soft laugh. "Do you mean that poem?"

Elizabeth nodded. "When I stepped out of the bookstore, my thoughts and emotions swirled within me, and I thought of her poem. I realized that every one of the descriptions of being in love was what I had just experienced when I was with him."

"You know it is love," Jane began, "when you catch the twinkle in his eyes but cannot catch your breath."

Elizabeth continued, "You feel a blush in your cheeks, and your knees feel weak."

Jane pondered for a moment and then said, "Your heart gives a shudder, and your mind is in a flutter."

They both smiled and said, "That is when you know it is love."

Elizabeth grasped both of Jane's hands. "I felt all those things, Jane. I now remember that I had stepped out of the bookstore and was looking down at the card and recollected that poem. I suddenly realized that I loved him! That is all I could think of! I was elated, excited, and filled with more joy than I have ever felt!"

Jane smiled. "You do truly love him!"

Elizabeth released her sister's hands and turned. "Yes. But at that moment, I slipped. I remember my foot suddenly going out from under me, and I tried futilely to grasp something to prevent my falling." She shook her head. "I could not catch myself and I tumbled down the step. The next thing I knew I was waking up in our aunt and uncle's home, unaware of anything that happened that day." She let out a low moan. "And it was three days later."

"I am grateful you finally remember, but I wish there was something I could do."

"There is nothing to be done now. In time, dearest Jane, I will be able to explain to him what happened, but only so he does not think ill of me." Tears began to spill down her cheeks, and her breath hitched. "I do not hold any hope... none whatsoever... that he would want to renew his affections to one who is so afflicted, who is unable to walk in an elegant manner..." She let out a long breath. "Or unable to accompany him onto the dance floor." She reached for a handkerchief and dabbed her eyes. "No, he is lost to me forever."

~~*

Darcy felt unsettled, but for the past few weeks, he had done his best to hide it from his sister. He could not rid himself of the irreconcilable feelings and thoughts he had about Elizabeth Bennet. The woman he believed her to be and the woman she had revealed in her behaviour were in stark contrast.

He paced about his London study, his hands clasped behind him, his gaze on the floor. His friend was to be married in but two days, and he should be there to support him in this joyous wedding celebration, but because of her, he could not. He had already written to Charles and apologized for not being able to attend.

He was packed and ready to set off for Rosings the following day, despite having recently heard from his cousin, Richard, that he was not able to join him. That would make it more difficult for him to endure his aunt's domineering and often caustic personality, as well as her ridiculous claims that he must marry her daughter, Anne. He now wished he had an excuse not to go.

He kicked an invisible obstacle out of his way and clenched his fists. He had chosen what he thought had been the lesser of two evils in deciding to visit his aunt instead of going to the wedding and encountering Elizabeth. Now, however, he doubted the sense of that decision.

He had thought he would be able to put Elizabeth out of his heart and mind by now. Despite all the rational arguments against her, he could not forget her. Perhaps he should have made one more attempt to...

"No!"

He slumped down in his chair and gazed down at the book on his desk. He picked it up and then promptly set it down. It no longer held any interest for him. He looked over at a stack of correspondence, knowing he should respond to them. He had at the least five invitations to balls and dinner parties, none of which he wished to attend. He could only imagine the young ladies at these affairs who would throw themselves at him.

He let out a huff. Elizabeth had never exhibited such behaviour and had challenged the very essence of his character. She had challenged him, defied him, and took great delight in countering his opinions. He had found her stimulating, refreshing, and... He let out a long sigh. "Beautiful," he said softly.

He turned in his chair, glancing out the window. It was a pleasant day outside, he determined to get out of the house. Perhaps he would encounter some lovely lady who did not know who he was, and they would discover they had much in common.

She would sing and play beautifully, love to take walks, speak with intelligence and grace, and... "She would love to read."

He stood up with determination and purpose. "I know where I shall go. I know where I must go!"

He passed Georgiana in the hall. "I shall be out for a while, Georgiana." He grabbed his hat and coat and smiled at her.

"Where are you going?" She tilted her head at him.

"I shall probably take a drive around St. James Park and then..." He paused and straightened up. "I plan to go to Cryderman's Bookstore."

"Indeed?" Georgiana's eyes widened. "Do you think that is wise?"

"I hope to find a good book to read." He placed a hand on her shoulder. "Fear not, Georgiana. I do not expect to encounter Miss Elizabeth again."

"I would like to accompany you, but I promised Eleanor Watkins that I would listen to her perform."

"Is she the daughter of the Watkins family who live a few houses away?"

"Yes. She is to perform at a soiree her parents are hosting later this month, and I fear she is a little nervous." Georgiana smiled. "It is her first time to perform."

Darcy's brows pinched. "I believe I have an invitation to that soiree on my desk."

"Do you plan to attend?"

Darcy winced. "I have not yet accepted. I had not really thought of it." He shifted from one foot to the other. "The only thing on my mind is having to leave for Rosings tomorrow, how long I shall have to stay, and how am I ever to survive without Richard there."

"So has that truly been the only thing on your mind?" She gave him a knowing look.

He did not answer, but only smiled.

"As I suspected. But if you do attend the soiree, Fitzwilliam, you will have to tell me how well she does."

"I am certain she will perform quite well if you took the time to assist her. She was wise to have asked you for your help, for I recollect the first time you performed in front of others. You almost ran out of the room when it was time to exhibit, yet you ended up performing splendidly."

"In truth, I still get nervous, but I just tell myself that as long as I have practiced and know the piece well, I have nothing to worry about."

"That is very good advice."

They walked to the door, and the butler opened it.

"Thank you, Hargrave." He turned back to Georgiana. "I hope you have an enjoyable time, and please give my regards to the Watkins family."

"I shall, and Brother?"

"Yes?"

"I hope... I hope you find a good book."

"Book?" He laughed. "Oh, yes. A book. I hope I do, as well.

~~*

Darcy had his driver circle St. James Park before setting out for the bookstore. It was a lovely day, and the spring flowers and tree blossoms painted a delightful picture. He wished he felt as serene on the inside as things looked on the outside.

When he pulled up in front of Cryderman's Bookstore, he felt his heart lurch. The last time he had visited and had walked out of the store, his heart had been soaring. How things had suddenly changed just four and twenty hours later.

He stepped from the carriage and hurried up the steps. He was determined to do two things while here. The first was to find a good book to read that would engage him, and the second was to put aside all memories of that encounter he had here with Elizabeth.

When he walked in, he was greeted by Mr. Cryderman. "Mr. Darcy! It is good to see you! It has been a while."

Darcy nodded. "Yes, I have been in Derbyshire for quite some time, and since returning to London, I have had other matters pressing on me."

The owner of the store pointed to a table of books. "There are some new titles we recently received. You might find something there to your liking."

Darcy thanked him, but instead of turning his gaze to the table, he looked towards the back of the store, where he and Elizabeth had stood talking. His mouth went dry, and he swallowed hard.

He walked over to the table and picked up a few of the newly released books, thumbing through them and then replacing them. He finally found one that looked like it might be something that would engage him and brought it over to the counter.

"Ah!" Mr. Cryderman said. "This book has been very well received. I believe you will enjoy it."

Darcy smiled. "Thank you. I hope I will, as well." He paid for the book and waved Mr. Cryderman off when he began to wrap it. "No need for that. I shall most likely begin reading it right away."

"As you wish, sir. As always, I thank you for your patronage." He handed him the book.

"It is my pleasure."

"Good afternoon, Mr. Darcy!"

Darcy turned to see Mrs. Cryderman step in. "Good afternoon, Mrs. Cryderman."

"It is good to see you. I hope you have been well."

"I have," he said. "And yourself?"

"I am well, indeed, but..."

Darcy gave her a questioning look when she did not finish.

"I wondered... how is that young lady faring after her fall?"

"Pardon? Young lady?"

Mrs. Cryderman gave an apologetic smile. "Forgive me for prying, Mr. Darcy, but the young lady who was in here talking with you the last time you were here." She pointed to the back of the store. "I have thought about her often, wondering if she has improved at all."

Darcy's brows lowered as he attempted to comprehend her comment. "I am sorry, but I fear I do not understand... What do you mean improved?"

"Oh, I am so sorry. I thought you would have known. When the young lady stepped out that day after you departed, she slipped on some ice on the steps and took a bad fall. She hit her head and twisted her foot quite severely."

Darcy's mouth dropped, and he could barely form a single thought. "I... I had no idea."

"She had mentioned to us that her aunt and uncle were across the street being fitted for clothes, so I rushed over to get them." A look of distress covered her face. "We could not waken her. It was terribly frightening. They took her immediately to their home and sent for a physician. I asked them to please let me know how she was doing. We were so grieved that it happened in front of our store."

"And did you ever find out what happened... what happened to her?" Darcy's heart pounded as he waited for her to reply.

"Her aunt wrote a few days later, and then they came back once, several weeks later. Apparently, her foot was severely injured. Not broken, I believe, but possibly a fracture." She looked down, shaking her head. "It is very difficult for her to even walk."

Darcy braced his hands on the counter as he thought back to seeing her seated at her home with a coverlet across her lap. That was why she had not agreed to go out for a walk! He suddenly felt a shudder pass through him! That was why she had not come to his home the following day. He only wished now that he could have spoken to her at Longbourn! He turned his gaze to the back of the store again, recollecting the encounter.

"But it is the other injury that has been so distressing."

Darcy quickly turned his head, his mouth dry. "What... what injury is that?"

"Her aunt told me that because of her head injury, it took her three days to wake up, and she has no memory of anything that happened that day. It is all completely gone!"

Darcy drew back. A myriad of thoughts and feelings assaulted him. He felt his chest constrict, making it difficult to even take a breath. He stood silent for a moment attempting to steady himself, then nodded and mouthed a 'thank you' as he walked numbly from the store, raking his fingers through his hair as he did.

When he reached his carriage, he curtly directed his driver to take him directly home. Once he was settled inside, he dropped his head against the back of the seat and closed his eyes. He had to force himself to take each breath.

"Dearest Elizabeth!" He slowly shook his head and gripped his hands tightly together. "Why did this happen to you? How could I have ever doubted you and your character?"

He lifted his head to gaze out the window. He saw nothing pass by but only an image of Elizabeth, sitting in a chair with a blanket covering her lap. Would she ever be able to walk again? Would she ever remember the pleasant encounter that they had enjoyed?

Chapter 13

Darcy handed off his coat, hat, and gloves to the butler as he hurried into his home, colliding with his sister as he did.

"Pray, excuse me, Georgiana."

He called his valet, and when Warrington arrived, he said, "Pack my bags, please, enough for at least two weeks, and keep out clothes suitable for a wedding. I will wear them when I leave in the morning."

Georgiana looked at him incredulously. "You will be wearing fine clothes to travel to Rosings?" She shook her head. "I know our aunt is particular about many things, but does she truly expect you to be dressed in clothes fit for a wedding when you arrive?"

He drew in a deep breath and placed his hands on her shoulders. "I am not going to Rosings." He paused and said softly, "I am going to Bingley's wedding."

Her jaw dropped, and her eyes opened wide. "Fitzwilliam Reginald Darcy! Will you never learn? You must accept that Miss Elizabeth Bennet's feelings for you are not what yours are for her and walk away! I know it is difficult, but..."

He leaned over and kissed her cheek, preventing her from continuing. "I learned something today that has changed everything."

She tilted her head. "Pray, what could you have learned that would change everything?"

"I shall explain in due time, but if we are to get to Hertfordshire in time for Bingley's wedding tomorrow, we must be ready to depart early in the morning." He leaned towards her. "You do wish to go, do you not? Do you wish to meet Miss Elizabeth Bennet?"

Georgiana excitedly clasped her hands together. "Truly, Brother? You wish for me to accompany you?"

"Indeed! Have your maid begin packing, and I shall see you in an hour in the parlour and explain everything."

She placed her hand on his arm. "But Brother, you know I must return the following day. As a thank you for helping Miss Watkins practice, her family has arranged a small gathering with her friends." She inclined her head. "I do not suppose you will want to return with me."

He looked down, shaking his head. "I cannot guarantee anything, but I hope... I hope I will be staying longer than just one day."

She reached up and kissed his cheek. "Mrs. Annesley shall accompany us, so if you discover Miss Bennet is receptive to your being there, and you do not wish to leave Hertfordshire – and I do hope you do not – she will return with me to London."

He watched Georgiana, her wide smile apparent, hurry away. He then proceeded up the stairs to his chambers. He took them slowly, wondering as he took each step whether anything had really changed. It was likely she did not remember their encounter. How would he reassure her that the last time they had met, it had been amicable between them? They had forgiven each other, spoken cordially to one another, and she had even accepted an invitation to his home.

He brought himself to a stop; his mouth was suddenly dry and his chest tight. His hand grasped the handrail tightly. There was no guarantee that she would be receptive to him this time, but...

"I must do this! I must see this through to the end... whatever the outcome may be!"

~~*

Later, as Darcy sat with Georgiana in the parlour, she listened in rapt attention as he explained what Mrs. Cryderman had told him. She remained silent until he had finished.

"So, Miss Bennet was unable to come to our home because she was injured and not conscious, and then likely did not recollect the encounter with you and your invitation when she awakened!"

Darcy gave a slow nod of his head.

"My goodness! This does change everything!"

"That was my thought. I hope it does."

She looked down at her clasped hands as she considered this. Her brows creased. "But do you suppose she still has no memory of that day? When you saw her in Hertfordshire, do you think she recollected your meeting? Could her memory have returned?"

"As I think back, I am quite certain she did not recall it. The expression on her face was not welcoming." He began to rub his jaw. "I believe she assumed I was still angry with her for refusing my offer." He tapped his fingers on the arm of the chair. "After all, in her mind, that was the last time we saw each other."

Georgiana reached over and placed her hand over his. "But what will this mean if she does not remember meeting you in the bookstore?"

Darcy paused and cast his glance down. "I am not certain, but I have every hope that since she was willing to forgive me and accept my forgiveness once, that she will be inclined to do so again." He lifted his eyes to his sister. "I can only hope that is the case."

Georgiana squeezed his hand. "I hope so, too." She gave him a sly smile. "So, you will not be going to Rosings as you had planned?"

He rolled his eyes and leaned his head back. "No, and that means I must write our aunt and convey my apology." He shook his head. "She will not be pleased."

Georgiana chuckled. "Is she ever pleased with anything?"

"I think not, Georgiana. I think not." He smiled. "But to own the truth, at the moment, I care little about how she will feel when she discovers that I will not be coming."

~~*

The Bennet's home was full; the Gardiners and their children had come from London, as well as Mr. Bennet's sister and family from the north. It was always enjoyable to gather with the family, but Elizabeth was grateful for the time she was able to spend alone with Mrs. Gardiner and Jane the evening before the wedding. The three ladies had a wonderful time conversing together.

Their aunt gave Jane some prudent advice on marriage. When she mentioned the poem she had taught the girls, Elizabeth determined it was the right time to share with her about all that had transpired between Mr. Darcy and herself, including his proposal, her refusal, their encounter in the bookstore, and his coming to Longbourn before her memory had returned.

Mrs. Gardiner was astonished to hear that the master of Pemberley had asked for her niece's hand in marriage and did not fully understand her reasons for refusing him until Elizabeth further explained. She also regretted that events had transpired that were keeping them apart.

"There is no need to feel regret, Aunt Gardiner. It is certainly no fault of yours."

"Perhaps you will have an opportunity to speak with him today. Will he not be standing up for Mr. Bingley?"

Elizabeth glanced down and shook her head. "He was unable to come. He is visiting his aunt in Kent."

Jane explained to her aunt. "Mr. Arnold, a young man who was acquainted with Charles and is now visiting his aunt and uncle here, is to stand up for him."

Her aunt took Elizabeth's hand. "I see. I am sorry I will not finally meet the gentleman. But Lizzy, perhaps in time he will come to hear of what happened to you, and he will understand."

Elizabeth wiped away a tear that escaped down her cheek. "I am not holding onto any hope that he would wish to pour out his affections on me again in my broken state."

"You are not broken!" both Jane and her aunt exclaimed.

Elizabeth drew in a shaky breath. "But I am. He lives in a world of fine, fashionable ladies, exquisite ballrooms, and those who have a critical eye for anything that does not meet their high standards." She clasped her hands together to keep them from shaking. "After having seen Pemberley and its beauty and majesty, I am convinced it requires a Mistress who will grace its halls with charm and dignity." She gave her head a shake. "I am not that person."

Mrs. Gardiner reached out for Elizabeth's hand. Her eyes narrowed, revealing a few wrinkles above her brow. A look of compassion then softened her features. "Elizabeth, how you must have experienced countless thoughts and emotions that day we walked through the different rooms and halls of Pemberley."

Elizabeth gave her aunt's hand a squeeze. "Indeed, I did." She drew in a raspy breath, wiping away another tear. "It was impossible to view the home with impartiality, especially as the housekeeper was so generous with her praise of Mr. Darcy. When we walked down the gallery of portraits, I felt a great sense of loss upon seeing his." She shrugged and attempted to smile. "I felt as though I had come home, but unfortunately, the truth I had to face was that... it was not my home... and likely never would be."

Jane wrapped her arm about her. "Oh, Lizzy, I had no idea you had felt that way."

Elizabeth leaned her head on Jane's shoulder and closed her eyes. "When we walked past the library, and I peeked inside, I realized I had never seen anything so beautiful. The house... the grounds... everything was finer than I could have ever imagined."

"I wondered why you had been so quiet, Lizzy. I thought you would have been more lavish in your praise of the home."

"I felt that if I praised the home too much, perhaps Mr. Darcy would come to hear of it. I feared him learning of my admiration for his home as much as I feared encountering him in it."

"Now I understand. I only wish I had known at the time. It must have been difficult to see..." Mrs. Gardiner paused.

Elizabeth tried to smile. "To see what could have been mine? I own that for days after, I found myself thinking of my first view of the beautiful manor, walking into every room, and what it would be like to explore the grounds and woods." She let out a long breath as she looked again at her aunt and sister. "I could not help but wonder what it would have been like to be Mistress of Pemberley."

"Did you feel any regret?" her aunt asked.

"Only a little, for I still had some doubts as to Mr. Darcy's character, his pride..." She pressed her lips tightly together. "There were some actions he had taken that still upset me."

"What actions?" Jane asked.

"It no longer matters. The truth is any regret I felt then is greatly surpassed by what I feel now." A smile suddenly touched

Elizabeth's lips. "But let us no longer dwell on what might have been. Tomorrow is the day we celebrate your wedding, Jane, and let us now only speak of that."

~~*

The next morning, Elizabeth sat on her bed and shook her head as the noise from downstairs continued unabated. It was mainly her mother's boisterous clamouring that dominated the tumult, but Lydia's wailing did not help. Her youngest sister was not happy with her dress, her hair, and some other complaint that Elizabeth could not discern.

Despite the noise that thundered unabated throughout the house, Elizabeth could smile. Today, after all, Jane was to marry the young man who had been in her heart for over a year and a half. Even when he left Netherfield and they had been uncertain whether he would ever return, her love and regard for him had remained steadfast.

She looked at herself in the mirror, satisfied with her appearance. She could not avoid looking down at her foot and hoping it would not cause her any discomfort as she stood at Jane's side. She was not so much worried about standing motionless on it during the ceremony, but it was walking up the aisle in the beginning and then back down at the end that had her concerned. She would have to concentrate on each step, making every attempt to not stumble and not wince from pain.

Elizabeth was grateful she would be walking back up the aisle on Mr. Arnold's arm. She knew she could trust him to be a support to her if she needed it. She looked down and wiggled her foot, which produced some shooting pain, causing her to flinch.

Jane peeked in with a wide smile. "Elizabeth, may we speak?"

Elizabeth quickly looked up and smiled at the radiant bride before her. "Oh, Jane, you are beautiful! Come in."

"Thank you. I wanted to do this one last time." Jane glanced about the room.

Elizabeth gave her a quizzical look. "Do what?"

"I wanted to come in and talk as we have done all our lives." Her eyes began to well with tears.

Elizabeth stretched out her arms and drew her sister into an embrace. "It is true that things are going to be different, but I am certain you will be able to share what is on your heart with your husband."

"I believe he will be a sympathetic listener, but I will so miss coming in here to talk with you."

"Well, I am only three miles away. I give you leave to come to Longbourn at any time if you want to talk." Elizabeth smiled and drew back. "You must promise me you will visit often."

"I promise, and you are invited to Netherfield, as well, without needing an invitation!"

Elizabeth tilted her head. "Mrs. Jane Bingley of Netherfield. That is going to take a while to flow naturally in conversation."

Jane chuckled. "I have been practicing saying it for some time, for I would not wish to make a mistake."

There was silence for a moment, and then Jane softly said, "Lizzy, how is your foot feeling today? Do you think you will be all right standing during the ceremony?"

"There is no need for you to worry. Now, my dearest sister, I think it is about time to leave for the church. Are you ready?"

Jane smiled. "I believe I am, Lizzy. I truly believe I am."

Elizabeth kissed her sister on the cheek, and the two left the room.

Chapter 14

Early the following morning, Darcy and Georgiana sat alone in the dining room as they waited to depart for the wedding. Georgiana was eating a hearty breakfast of ham, eggs, and fruit, while Darcy had little appetite and only took an occasional bite of a biscuit and slowly sipped his coffee.

Darcy spoke of the clear blue sky, soft breeze, and mild temperatures that would make their journey a promising one, and Georgiana commented on the chorus of birds serenading them with their songs, and where and when they might make brief stops along the way. They spoke of everything save for Miss Elizabeth Bennet.

Darcy was fatigued from nerves that had plagued him throughout the night. There were a few times he considered cancelling the trip altogether, but directly after having engaged that thought, his heart had felt heavy, and he determined it was something he had to do.

At length, after avoiding the subject throughout the meal, Georgiana brought up her concern over her brother's apparent unease.

"Fitzwilliam, you have barely eaten anything this morning. Are you unwell?" She leaned in towards him. "Are you having second thoughts about seeing... Miss Bennet?"

Darcy turned away and glanced out the window. He looked back at his sister and began to rub his jaw. "I have such a mixture of anticipation and anxiety, excitement and exhaustion over just the thought of seeing her again. I have never..." His voice trailed off.

Georgiana stood up and walked around the table, taking the

chair next to him. "Fitzwilliam, what is it about Miss Elizabeth Bennet that has captivated you so? I truly wish to know."

Her slight, mischievous smile disarmed him. "She is everything I ever..." He stopped and shook his head, letting out a chuckle. "No, she is nothing like any woman I imagined I would fall in love with."

"In what way?"

Darcy faced her. "In so many ways. I never thought I would meet a woman so intelligent and witty, who is not afraid to challenge me and speak the truth to me." He paused and drew in a long breath. "She is beautiful in appearance and a pleasure to behold, but more than that, she is kind, caring, generous..." His voice trailed off.

"She sounds lovely."

Darcy smiled. "We have been apart for long lengths of time, but during all those times, I..." He pressed his lips together as he pondered how to explain this to his sister, when he did not fully understand it himself. "Even though we were apart, she was always with me."

"What do you mean?"

Darcy took his time answering. "I would hear her soft, lilting voice at unexpected times. Her beautiful eyes and smile would flash before me. I would see something and think she would enjoy seeing it and sharing the view with me." His brows pinched. "At Pemberley, whenever I walked the grounds, I thought how much she would enjoy walking through them, and I wondered what it would be like to have her walking alongside me... with her hand in mine."

Georgiana smiled. "And you had no idea when you returned to Pemberley after seeing her in town that she had toured the house and looked out on the grounds. It is unfortunate she had not been able to walk through them because of the rain."

His slow nod suddenly stopped, and his eyes widened. "Rain! Last year it was raining the day I arrived back at Pemberley. That could very well have been the day they toured the house!"

"Oh, Brother! Can you imagine if you had encountered her that day?" She smiled broadly. "What would you have done if you had seen her there?"

He did not answer immediately. Finally, he said, "I doubt very much that I would have believed my eyes. I would have thought I was seeing an apparition, that she was merely a dream." He raked his fingers through his hair. "I hope that I would have been able to overcome my shock and make every attempt to display to her that I was a changed man after taking her honest view of my character and its imperfections to heart."

There was silence between the two for a few moments, and then Georgiana finally said, "She sounds wonderful, Fitzwilliam. She is a woman who..." The young girl chuckled. "She is a woman who – without even trying – has made you a better man. I cannot wait to meet her."

~~*

Darcy and Georgiana, along with Mrs. Annesley, left London as the sun was just peering over the horizon. They anticipated a pleasant journey, as there were no indications of inclement weather. As he had when he left Pemberley for Hertfordshire, he tethered his horse behind the carriage.

They were dressed in the clothes they would be wearing to the wedding. Darcy's plan was to stop at the inn in Meryton and secure two rooms, freshen up, and then set out for the church. He wanted to be able to assure Caroline Bingley – as well as her brother – that they had already secured accommodations if either were to ask. He was certain Miss Bingley would insist they stay at Netherfield. The last thing he wanted was to put himself or his sister within the clutches of that woman.

Darcy and Georgiana each brought a book to read, and Mrs. Annesley brought some needlework. For the most part there was silence as they journeyed, save for an occasional comment about the passing scenery, an inquiry when they might stop next, or Georgiana asking her brother about the neighbourhood around Meryton.

They finally came into Hertfordshire and drew nearer to the small village of Meryton. Darcy felt himself growing impatient. He glanced down at his watch often to check the time. When it became apparent they might not arrive at the church on time, he became restless, tapping his fingers on the side of the carriage or letting out a long sigh.

He caught Georgiana watching him and gave her a reassuring smile that he was doing well. In truth, however, he could barely sit still.

The carriage finally pulled onto the main street of Meryton and came to a stop in front of the inn.

Darcy pulled out his watch and let out a groan, seeing that the wedding was to begin in half an hour. They would have to hurry if they were to make it to the church on time. They all stepped from the carriage and walked into the inn as the footmen began to unload their belongings.

When they stepped into the parlour, they found it empty. Darcy walked over to a desk and rang the bell. He fidgeted nervously as he waited for someone to appear.

At length, an elderly gentleman shuffled into the room. He straightened his glasses and his neck cloth as he greeted his guests.

"Do you have a reservation?" he asked.

Darcy shook his head. "No, we only discovered we were coming yesterday. We just need two small rooms, preferably next to each other, but being close will suffice."

"Well," the old man began, "We only have six rooms, and if you do not have a reservation, I regret that I cannot give you one. They have all been taken."

Darcy looked back at his sister and her companion. They watched him intently.

He turned back to the proprietor. "Is there another inn nearby? Some other place we can secure accommodations?"

"Well, there is an inn six miles back down the main road. I cannot guarantee they have any rooms available, let alone speak for the quality of the place, but it is the closest."

Darcy looked at his watch. The wedding would begin shortly. "Would you have a room available in which the ladies could freshen up? I will gladly pay for their use of it."

"Well, we do have guests coming in later today. I can let the ladies use their room. We should have enough time to get it ready afterwards for those guests."

Darcy thanked the gentleman and then escorted the ladies to

the room. He stepped outside to instruct his men to reload their belongings back onto the carriage, then returned to the parlour and waited for the ladies to finish. When they were done, he would make use of the room, and then they would set off for the church.

Once they were settled back in the carriage and on their way to the church, Darcy wanted nothing more than to sit back and relax, but he could not. He hoped his forthcoming encounter with Elizabeth would go much more smoothly than his attempt to get a room at the Meryton Inn and arrive at the church on time. As it was, they would be several minutes late, which Darcy hated. He always insisted on being punctual himself, and to be late to his best friend's wedding he considered inexcusable. To delay seeing Elizabeth, he deemed insupportable.

~~*

Elizabeth stood at the back of the church with Jane, waiting for the moment they would walk down the aisle. Jane's hand was already tucked about her father's arm. Mr. Bennet nervously shifted his weight from one foot to the other.

"Lizzy, how are you feeling?" Jane asked. "Shall you be able to walk up the aisle without difficulty?"

Elizabeth smiled. "Without difficulty? Yes. With the elegance and air of a fine lady, unfortunately, no." She placed her hand on Jane's and gave it a squeeze. "You have no need to worry about me. The only thing you need to concern yourself about is whether you will remember to answer the clergyman's questions at the right time... and with the correct answer."

"Now, Lizzy," Mr. Bennet began. "Our Jane will do superbly." He chuckled. "But I cannot be so confident about Mr. Bingley."

Jane gave her father's hand a playful pat, and then looked to her sister when the church bells pealed. "I believe it is time to walk in."

Elizabeth smiled. "So it is." She leaned over and kissed her sister. "Just think, dearest Jane. When you walk out of this church, you will be Mrs. Bingley!"

She turned, and with care and careful determination, she began to walk down the aisle towards the front. Heads were turned, but they were not so much watching her, but watching for the bride. That is what she thought until she came upon Miss Bingley, who seemed to inspect her with a look of disdain. As much as she tried to walk gracefully, she knew she had a slight limp.

She turned to Mr. Bingley and smiled. He was standing upright and stiff, with an eager, but nervous smile on his face.

She glanced at Mr. Arnold, who appeared much more relaxed.

He gave her a smile and a slight nod, as if to encourage her that she was walking well and only had a little further to go. When she tried to smile back, however, she had the sudden thought — and greatest wish — that it was Mr. Darcy standing at Mr. Bingley's side. She felt a great sense of regret that he would not be here today.

Chapter 15

Elizabeth stood at Jane's side watching the beautiful, radiant, and joyful bride as she and Mr. Charles Bingley exchanged vows.

While the service was not particularly long, the pain in Elizabeth's foot became more intense, and she frequently lifted it off the ground, balancing precariously on her other foot. She hoped no one noticed and was grateful she would have Mr. Arnold's arm to cling to as she walked back up the aisle.

At the conclusion of the ceremony, the newly married couple turned to face their guests and proceeded to walk back up the aisle. They wore wide smiles that displayed their delight to all.

Elizabeth took slow, cautious steps as she came to Mr. Arnold's side and wrapped her fingers about his arm.

He looked down and smiled. "Hold on tightly. We will take it slow."

Elizabeth murmured, "Thank you."

Out of the corner of her eye, she again noticed Miss Bingley's raised brow and insipid smile as her eyes travelled down to her foot. If Elizabeth had been able, and if she had not been at her sister's wedding with all eyes upon her, she would have stamped that foot down hard at that woman's audacity. Even if it hurt!

They began walking, and Mr. Arnold encouraged her. "We do not have that far to go. Just a few more steps. You are doing superbly."

Elizabeth looked up and whispered back, "Thank you. I am trying, but it is taking an effort. I..." She paused and happened to glance to her right, where another pair of eyes were upon her.

Mr. Darcy!

Elizabeth was so taken aback that her step faltered. If it had not been for the firm support of Mr. Arnold, who immediately grasped her with his other hand, she would have stumbled in front of everyone. She was certain everyone noticed, as Mr. Darcy began to reach out as if to catch her.

She tried to smile but could not. She was barely mindful of how to take a step that would not result in another mishap. She brought her other hand firmly around Mr. Arnold's arm for more support.

When they finally reached the back of the church, Mr. Arnold looked down. "What happened back there, Miss Bennet? Are you all right? How is your foot?"

His eyes were kind, but she saw they were also questioning.

Elizabeth released his arm and made a futile attempt to laugh about the incident. "My foot must have fallen asleep from standing for so long, and I believe I misjudged my step."

She had no idea whether she was making any sense, for her mind was in turmoil. What was Mr. Darcy doing here?

A mixture of both anticipation and apprehension began to flood her. She was grateful she would finally be able to explain the reason for not coming to his home, but upon seeing her condition, he would likely want nothing more to do with her. And he certainly would have every reason now to consider her damaged, and not suitable to even consider her to be his wife and the Mistress of Pemberley. So much had changed since their encounter in the bookstore, when she had hoped he might renew his addresses. If it had not been for her injury, she certainly would have received them wholeheartedly.

The couple followed Charles and Jane as they made their way to the vestry to sign the parish book. As they waited for the clergyman to join them, Elizabeth drew her sister into a warm embrace.

"Congratulations, Mrs. Bingley. I am so happy for you!"

"Oh, thank you, Lizzy. How are you faring?"

Elizabeth chuckled. "I am doing well, except for slightly faltering as we walked back up the aisle."

Jane's face fell. "I am so sorry. Are you hurt?"

"No, thank goodness, and there is no need to be sorry. It was nothing." She glanced up at Mr. Arnold. "I do thank Mr. Arnold, however, for keeping me up on my feet and secure."

Bingley slapped Arnold on the back. "Good for you! I knew you would make a splendid best man. But did you see Darcy was here? He actually came! I was surprised, as I was not expecting to see him at all!"

Elizabeth silently agreed with his sentiments, and she met her sister's questioning glance with a slight nod.

The clergyman stepped in and directed everyone to the parish book. He gave directions where each person was required to sign and then presented a copy to the couple for safe keeping.

Once they finished, they stepped out of Longbourn church and walked to the carriage that would convey them to Netherfield for the wedding breakfast. Others were already on their way. Elizabeth and Mr. Arnold walked slowly, and again she was grateful that he was being so mindful of her injury. She guardedly looked about for Mr. Darcy but did not see him. He must have already departed.

As they made their way to Netherfield, Elizabeth was quiet while the two men conversed incessantly. Never in her life had she been more unsettled or felt such uncertainty, but she was surprised there was also a tinge of hope. She could not pay attention to the conversation, as all she could think was that Mr. Darcy was here.

When they arrived at the Bingleys' home, Mr. Arnold carefully assisted Elizabeth out of the carriage. They walked into Netherfield, and upon entering the ballroom, she again looked about for Mr. Darcy.

She saw him at once across the room. He stood with a young lady who had blond hair and a youthful innocence about her. She realized he had been seated next to her in the church pew but had given no thought to who she was in the moment before she stumbled. She pondered whether it might be his sister.

She needed to talk to him, but she preferred to do it without Mr. Arnold at her side. Fortunately, he provided the perfect opportunity, himself. "Miss Bennet, I will escort you to a chair so you may sit and rest your foot. I see my aunt and uncle across the room. If you do not mind, I shall go speak to them."

He brought her to a chair, and once she sat, he asked, "Would you care for something to eat or drink, first?"

"No, thank you, but I appreciate the offer."

When Mr. Arnold walked away, Elizabeth felt a small thrill of hope when she saw Mr. Darcy walk towards her. He came up and gave a slight bow, and they both began to speak at once.

"Mr. Darcy, I..."

"Miss Bennet..."

They chuckled at their simultaneous greeting. Elizabeth clasped her hands. "Please, allow me to speak, Mr. Darcy. I owe you an apology and an explanation why my aunt and uncle and I did not come to your house in London after you so graciously invited us, and I will not rest until you allow me to do so."

Darcy shook his head. "You have no need to explain or to apologize, for I only recently came to learn of what happened to you."

Elizabeth was stunned. "You know? How did you learn of it?"

Darcy smiled. "Mrs. Cryderman at the bookstore told me. I went in..." He paused. "It seems like an eternity ago, but it was just yesterday. I went into the bookstore, and she inquired as to how you were. I had no idea of what she was speaking, and so she informed me as to the circumstances when you left the shop that day."

Elizabeth smiled. "Dear Mrs. Cryderman. She was so very concerned for me that she insisted my aunt keep her apprised of my condition." She looked down at her foot. "She explained to you how I fell and injured my foot?"

Darcy gave a slow nod of his head.

"And did she... did she tell you anything else?"

"She did." Darcy drew in a breath. "She informed me that you hit your head, were unconscious for several days, and when you awoke, you had no memory of that whole day."

"That is why we did not come... why we were unable to come." She felt tears threaten to fill her eyes. "Since my aunt and uncle were unaware of the invitation you extended to us, they had no way to know they should have sent you a letter explaining our absence. When I finally awoke, I had no memory of it." She let out a long sigh. "I can only imagine what you must have thought when we did not arrive."

Darcy felt a stab of regret at the myriad thoughts he had of her in the weeks and months following. "I began to wonder whether I had imagined the whole thing." He tried to smile. "When did you recall the events of that day?"

"About a week ago. I was looking through my reticule and found your card. I could not understand why it was in my purse and what it meant. Suddenly, it all came back to me."

"How are you now? How is your foot?"

Elizabeth was encouraged by his concern and the look of genuine compassion apparent on his face.

She tried to make light of her feelings. "Well, you saw how I nearly fell when I was leaving the church after the wedding." She let out a soft, resigned breath. "I am not altogether healed." She looked up into his rich, brown eyes, and she found it difficult to pull hers away. "The physician says I may likely... I may never be completely healed." There, she had said it. He would understand.

There was silence for a moment. His eyes darkened, and he said, "I am sorry. I hope he is wrong."

"Thank you. As do we all."

Darcy looked about, and Elizabeth was certain he was trying to determine a polite way to take his leave.

Looking at the newly married couple, he asked, "Are Charles and your sister to take a wedding journey?"

"Yes, they will leave for the southern coast immediately after the cake is served."

"I see. I need to offer them my congratulations before they depart."

"Yes." Elizabeth's heart was heavy, and she expected him to walk away, but instead, he turned back to her.

"Would you allow me to introduce you to my sister?"

Elizabeth was stunned, and she was certain it was reflected in her face. "Yes! I would... I would be delighted to meet her."

She felt a surge of elation as Mr. Darcy walked over to his sister. When they returned, he made the introductions.

Elizabeth smiled. "It is a pleasure to make your acquaintance, Miss Darcy."

"The pleasure is all mine," the young girl replied.

Mr. Darcy stood back watching while the two ladies conversed. Elizabeth delighted in Miss Darcy's company and felt regret that it might be the last time she would ever see her. She would have enjoyed becoming better acquainted with her.

"Are you staying here at Netherfield?" Elizabeth asked.

Miss Darcy looked at her brother, who answered. "No. We had hoped to stay at the Inn in Meryton, but they had no rooms available. The proprietor mentioned an inn six miles outside of town, but we had not time to go back and check for rooms there." He gave a shrug. "We were already going to be late for the wedding. We did not wish to risk missing it altogether."

Elizabeth frowned. "I know the inn of which he spoke, and I fear... I do not believe you would wish to stay there. Particularly you, Miss Darcy." She turned to Mr. Darcy. "The tavern there tends to get rather rough and boisterous late into the night."

Darcy pinched his brows. "Is there another inn nearby that might be more suitable?"

Elizabeth shook her head. "Unfortunately, no." She paused, and her eyes lit up. But I do have an idea." She looked back at Miss Darcy. "You would be more than welcome to stay at our house."

Mr. Darcy put up his hand. "I would expect your house is already full."

"Ah, yes. It is quite full, with many of our family here. There was not a single room available last night." She paused. "But there is a little fact you may not have considered."

Miss Darcy laughed softly. "What would that be?"

Elizabeth's brows lifted. "My sister Jane's room is now available. I can send word home to have it readied for you for this evening. You are welcome to stay as long as you wish." She turned to Mr. Darcy. "Unfortunately, we do not have an additional room for you, Mr. Darcy, so I fear you will have to stay at the other inn." She smiled. "I am certain it will not injure your sensibilities too much."

"I believe I am up to the task." He smiled and directed his gaze at Elizabeth. "As long as I know my sister is in good hands."

His look of appreciation and his complimentary words were another welcome surprise.

"Oh, but Miss Bennet, my companion is with me." Miss Darcy extended her hand to the edge of the room, where an older woman sat. "Mrs. Annesley will need a room, as well." A look of disappointment came upon her face. "I fear it will not work, after all."

"Hmm." Elizabeth pondered this momentarily, and then she smiled. "I have two beds in my room. You both can stay in there, and I will stay in Jane's room."

Miss Darcy smiled. "Or, if you do not mind, you and I can stay in your room, and Mrs. Annesley can stay by herself in your sister's room."

Elizabeth chuckled. "If you insist."

Their conversation was interrupted when Caroline Bingley came up to them.

"Mr. Darcy! Miss Darcy! You do not know how pleased I was to see that you came to the wedding!" She grasped the young girl's hands. "How did I not know you would be here?"

"Circumstances came to light only yesterday that prompted our decision to come," Mr. Darcy answered for his sister.

"I am delighted!" She turned to Elizabeth. "But how unfortunate that you nearly fell, Miss Bennet, as you walked back up the aisle. I do hope you were not injured any more severely than you already are."

Elizabeth grit her teeth through her smile. "I thank you for your concern, Miss Bingley, but there was no further injury."

"I am glad to hear that." She turned back to Mr. Darcy and his sister. "You are staying at Netherfield, of course. We have several fine rooms available!"

"We thank you, Miss Bingley," Miss Darcy said. "However, Miss Bennet has generously offered rooms at Longbourn."

Miss Bingley turned and glared at Elizabeth with a veiled smile. She turned back to Miss Darcy with an artificial smile and let out a chuckle. "Longbourn? How sweet of her. However, you must not feel compelled to stay there merely because she asked. You must stay with us at Netherfield. I will settle for nothing less. I am certain you will be much more comfortable here."

Chapter 16

Miss Darcy looked up at Miss Bingley and squared her shoulders. "I thank you, no." Her voice and expression were firm.

Both Elizabeth and Darcy were startled at the young girl's determination, while the colour drained from Miss Bingley's face. She muttered something unintelligible, excused herself, and immediately turned away.

Elizabeth lifted her brows and smiled mischievously at the young girl as she whispered, "From her expression, I would surmise she did not expect such a forceful refusal from you, Miss Darcy."

Georgiana blanched and put her fingers over her mouth. "Oh dear, was I terribly rude?" She looked at her brother. "I hope I did not speak unkindly."

"You were very polite, Georgiana. Do not concern yourself." He turned to Elizabeth. "If you will excuse us, we need to pay our respects to the newlyweds before they depart."

"Of course! I will send a note to Longbourn to have them ready both rooms, and I look forward to spending some time with you this evening." She took Miss Darcy's hand. "You and Mrs. Annesley may come to our home at any time."

Mr. Darcy and his sister turned and walked over to the newly married couple, leaving Elizabeth feeling great delight knowing she would be able to get to know Mr. Darcy's sister a little better. She enjoyed the young girl's company for the short amount of time they just spent together; however, the excitement of becoming better acquainted with her was dimmed by the knowledge that she may never see her again.

When they walked away, Elizabeth sat alone until Mr. Bennet

joined her.

"How are you faring, Lizzy?"

She smiled up at him. "I am well."

"Good," he replied, as he fingered his neck cloth, attempting to loosen it a bit. "I was worried about you when you began to fall. I was glad to see Mr. Arnold held you secure."

Elizabeth chuckled. "Yes, he performed admirably. I greatly appreciated his quick response."

"I noticed Mr. Darcy condescended to come and speak to you." He gave her a wink. "Was he critical of the way you walked – and then stumbled – in the aisle?"

"No, he was perfectly amiable." She glanced over at him. "He had recently learned of my fall and wanted to inquire how I was."

"What a fine gentleman!" He lifted his eyes toward the gentleman. "And who is that young lady with him? Is it his intended?" He shook his head. "She appears too young for him."

"No, Father. It is his sister." She lifted her hand. "Would you help me stand? I think it is about time to be seated for the breakfast, and I would like to avoid the crush."

Mr. Bennet brought Elizabeth to her feet, and they began to walk to the tables.

"Father, I have a favour to ask of you."

"Anything, my dear," he replied as he patted her hand.

"Could you please send a note home and ask that Hill ready both Jane's room and my room for guests?"

He turned to her, stunned. "We are to have more guests?"

"Yes, I offered Jane's room and mine to Miss Darcy and her companion. There was no room at the Inn at Meryton, and the only other inn is the one outside of town. I did not feel it was suitable for the young lady. I hope you do not mind."

"I do not, for it will not inconvenience me at all." He let out a laugh. "I am certain, however, your mother will have nervous fits of honour, excitement, and anxiety having such an esteemed young lady staying at our home." He looked down at Elizabeth. "You will inform her, will you not?"

"I will try to reassure her that there is no need to be concerned." She smiled up at him. "Miss Darcy is a very sweet girl."

"Ah, unlike her brother, is she?" He let out a huff. "I will believe it when I see it for myself."

Mr. Bennet seated Elizabeth at the table and then left to take care of her request.

When Mrs. Bennet sat down at the table across from her, Elizabeth had the opportunity to inform her that Miss Darcy and her companion would be staying the night at Longbourn. Just as her father had foreseen, her nerves began to flare with every imaginable emotion.

"Oh, such a lovely lady from a fine family! Oh, the honour! Everything must be in order! But will she find everything to her satisfaction? Oh! What must be done in preparation of her arrival?"

Elizabeth spoke softly and calmly to reassure her that everything was taken care of and there was no need for her to worry. She had determined she was going to do everything in her power to keep Miss Darcy from certain members of her family, particularly her mother and Lydia. Even if it meant sequestering themselves in her room the entirety of the time she was there.

When the Gardiners approached the table, Mrs. Gardiner came up behind Elizabeth and put her hands on her shoulders, leaning in. "I saw Mr. Darcy speaking with you. Is everything well between you? Were you able to explain our absence?"

Elizabeth gave her a reassuring nod. "Yes, everything is well." She looked up and smiled. "I will tell you about it later, but I do have some interesting news I must share with you."

"What is that?"

"Miss Darcy and her companion will be staying the night at Longbourn."

Mrs. Gardiner's eyes widened, and her jaw dropped in surprise. "What a delightful surprise! I cannot wait to hear how this came about." She gave Elizabeth's shoulders a squeeze. "And I cannot wait to become acquainted with the young lady!" She then walked to her place across the table from her.

When Charles and Jane took their seats to her left, Elizabeth briefly told her sister what had transpired between her and Mr. Darcy.

"I am glad you have things settled between you," Jane said as she took her sister's hand. "He is a good man." She gave her hand a squeeze.

Elizabeth silently nodded. She felt that any words spoken now would result in an onslaught of tears.

During the meal, there were many looks of love and encouragement exchanged between the two eldest sisters. Elizabeth felt such melancholy that things had now changed between them, despite being delighted for her at the same time.

She tried to dispel her feelings, reminding herself that Jane was only three miles from Longbourn, but she knew that part of her sadness was her realization of the good in Mr. Darcy and yet, how things had changed between them due to her injury.

As they ate the meal, Elizabeth had a view of Mr. Darcy and his sister, but she was not close enough to speak to them. Unfortunately for him, she saw that he was seated near Miss Bingley. Elizabeth could only imagine the conversation being carried on at the far end of the table.

After the meal, the cake was served, and there was a cheerful farewell to Charles and Jane as they departed for their wedding journey. Once they had taken their leave, Mr. Darcy approached Elizabeth.

"Again, I want to thank you for extending the invitation to my sister and Mrs. Annesley to stay the night at Longbourn. Was it acceptable to your parents?"

"It was. They are delighted to have them."

He gave a nod and smiled. "I am glad to hear that. I will bring them by shortly."

"You are welcome to come at any time."

~~*

When the Bennet family arrived back at Longbourn, Elizabeth was pleased to see that Hill had prepared the rooms for the guests. Everything appeared to be in order.

She was tired, and her foot ached, so she collapsed into a chair in the parlour next to her aunt. Most of the family rested in their rooms after the busy morning.

Elizabeth and her aunt watched the children play, somewhat

boisterously at times, while Mary attempted to keep them quiet. Having little success, Mary ended up holding the youngest on her lap and distracting her by reading a book to her.

At length, Mrs. Gardiner reached over and placed her hand on her niece's arm.

"Tell me, Lizzy, what did you tell Mr. Darcy, and what was his response?"

Elizabeth smiled. "I had no need to tell him anything."

"Truly? Why is that?"

Elizabeth explained to her how he had come to learn of her fall.

Mrs. Gardiner lifted her brows. "He came to learn of it just yesterday, did he? Is that the reason he decided to come to the wedding?" She leaned in towards Elizabeth, giving her a pointed look.

"I cannot answer that, for I did not ask him whether that was the reason." She shook her head. "Even if he did, seeing me as I am, lame and unsteady, I know he will not be renewing his addresses."

Her aunt clicked her tongue. "But consider how much he must thoroughly trust you to have allowed his sister to stay here the night."

Elizabeth smiled. "The other options they had were not particularly appealing."

At that moment, Mrs. Bennet walked in and sat down. She picked up her handkerchief and began to wave it in front of her face. "Oh, the children! Can they not play quietly? I was not able to rest at all!"

Elizabeth smiled. "They had to be calm and quiet for most of the morning, Mother. I believe they reached their limit!"

Mrs. Gardiner chuckled. "Indeed!"

Elizabeth let her head drop back, and she closed her eyes. If it were not for the eager anticipation of certain guests arriving, she could easily have drifted off to sleep – despite the noise of the children.

~~*

Hill appeared at the doorway and announced Mr. and Miss

Darcy and Mrs. Annesley. Elizabeth lifted her head, giving it a shake. Had she fallen asleep despite her determination not to do so? How long had she slept? The guests stepped into the room, and Elizabeth attempted to stand, only to feel a wave of dizziness sweep over her. She leaned over to grasp the arm of the chair.

"Please, Miss Bennet. Do not stand on our account." Mr. Darcy's voice was firm, yet kind.

She was grateful, for she was uncertain whether she would have been able to stand. She gave her head a slight shake to rid it of the fogginess of a short nap, and then made introductions.

Mrs. Bennet walked up. "We are delighted to host you here this evening, Miss Darcy and Mrs. Annesley. Please come in. I am certain you will be most comfortable. Hill, will you show the ladies to their rooms and have their belongings brought up?"

As the ladies walked away, Mr. Darcy came and stood in front of Elizabeth. "How are you feeling, Miss Bennet?"

"I am well, just a little tired."

"As is everyone, I am certain," Mr. Darcy replied. He looked over at Mrs. Gardiner. "I understand one of Miss Bennet's aunts grew up in Lambton. Might that be you?"

Mrs. Gardiner smiled. "Indeed, it is. I have fond memories of that little town, and more particularly, of your kind and generous parents and your wonderful home, Pemberley."

"Thank you. I appreciate that."

At that moment, two of Mrs. Gardiner's children began playing a little too rambunctiously, so she excused herself to go to them.

Mr. Darcy immediately sat down beside Elizabeth. She felt her cheeks grow warm, and it was difficult for her to even take a breath because of his nearness. Their shoulders brushed against each other, as did the sides of their shoes.

He looked a little nervous, while at the same time eager to speak. Finally, he said, "Miss Bennet, I have a confession I must make." He paused. "And I hope you will not despise me for it."

Chapter 17

Elizabeth nearly laughed at the notion that Mr. Darcy felt he needed to confess something to her. In fact, a laugh might dispel the feelings his nearness evoked. The distress on his face, however, prompted her to check her response. "Pray, what did you do, Mr. Darcy, that requires a confession?"

He leaned in even closer and spoke in a husky whisper. "You may have noticed that we sat near Miss Bingley during the wedding breakfast." When Elizabeth nodded, he began to rub his jaw. "She may be under the assumption that I..." He paused and drew in a breath. "She believes that I am also staying the night here at Longbourn, as well as my sister."

Elizabeth smiled at the thought of poor Miss Bingley trying to get a good night's sleep believing that to be true. She clasped her hands and shook her head. "Poor Miss Bingley! She cannot be pleased."

"I know it was very wrong of me, but I chose not to correct this misapprehension of hers." He shook his head. "I believed that if she knew I had not secured a room yet, she would insist I stay at Netherfield. I would do no such thing without her brother there, despite a multitude of other family members being there. I knew she would not relent."

"I imagine she would not," Elizabeth replied.

He looked up and met her eyes. "But I give you leave to correct her, if you choose." He paused and then added with a soft smile, "At some later date."

His eyes conveyed a warmth that she dared not consider. She could not assume anything presently, due to the strength of her feelings. "I will consider it, Mr. Darcy, but then again, I may allow her to continue in this misapprehension." She was rewarded with a broader smile. "Would you care to stay and visit with my family for a time? We will be eating shortly." She hoped he did not notice the crack in her voice.

"That is exceedingly kind of you, but I really ought to secure a room at the inn. I will return in the morning to send Georgiana and Mrs. Annesley back to London." He stood up.

Elizabeth looked up at him and smiled. "If you discover the inn does not have any rooms available, we have a comfortable sofa here you can sleep on."

It was a moment before he replied. "Thank you. I will consider it."

"Or, you could always accept Miss Bingley's offer, thus increasing her happiness at the risk of forfeiting your own."

He let out a laugh. "Your sofa, I believe, would be preferable." He looked up as Georgiana and Mrs. Annesley returned from their rooms.

He walked over to his sister and kissed the top of her head. "I will see you in the morning."

"Sleep well, Fitzwilliam."

"I will try!" He turned back to Elizabeth. "Goodbye, Miss Bennet, and again, I thank you."

After he left, Elizabeth was able to turn her attention to Miss Darcy and Mrs. Annesley. "We will be eating shortly, but are either of you in need of anything to eat or drink now?"

They both thanked her and declined.

"Come, sit down, and let us talk. I would like to get to know you better."

~~*

Mrs. Annesley kept to herself doing some needlework while Miss Darcy visited with those in the Bennet household. Elizabeth was pleased that both her mother and Lydia behaved themselves, and she credited herself for making an emphatic demand for calmness and polite conversation earlier in the day.

It was Kitty, however, who took a strong liking to the young girl. Elizabeth reasoned it was likely because they were closer in age, but she was delighted that her younger sister was maturing in the art of conversing.

They talked of the wedding, of course, London, the weather, places they would like to visit in England, and other inconsequential things that ladies talk about in polite conversation. They talked of everything save for the one thing Elizabeth wished to talk to Miss Darcy about – her brother.

Later that evening, Mrs. Annesley bid them goodnight; Kitty soon followed. Elizabeth and Georgiana, who were now on a first name basis, went up to Elizabeth's room and readied themselves for bed. Instead of crawling under the blankets, however, Georgiana sat on top of her bed and looked over at her new friend.

"Elizabeth, I want you to know how much I have enjoyed getting to know you... and Kitty... and your whole family. I want to thank you for the invitation you so graciously extended to Mrs. Annesley and me to stay here."

Elizabeth smiled. "It is my pleasure. I could not imagine you ladies spending the night at the inn." She chuckled. "I do hope your brother will be able to get some sleep."

Georgiana bit her lip. "He is a light sleeper. If it is as boisterous as you say, he may sleep very little."

Elizabeth leaned in towards her. "Is he terribly irritable in the morning if he does not get enough sleep?"

Georgiana shook her head. "Oh, no! Well, at least not that I have ever seen." She let out a soft laugh. "If he is at all provoked when he first wakes up, by the time I see him, he has probably regulated any negative feelings he had upon awakening." Shaking her head, she said, "I tend to wake up much later than he does."

"I tend to rise early," Elizabeth said. "If the weather is nice, I typically enjoy going outside for a long walk, often before anyone else is up. Except my father. He wakes earlier than I." Elizabeth suddenly grimaced and tossed her head. "Well, I used to get up and walk. I cannot take my long walks anymore."

"I am so sorry about your accident. Does the physician believe it will eventually heal?"

"Anything is possible, but if it is improving, it is certainly taking its time!" She looked down at her foot as she twirled it around.

"I hope it does," Georgiana said.

Elizabeth looked up and smiled. "As do I." She bit her lip and looked up. "I understand your brother will not be returning with you to London. Do you know what his plans are?"

Georgiana smiled. "No. I do not even think he is certain."

"Oh." Elizabeth chuckled. "I suppose he is one of those brothers who shares very little with their sisters."

"Oh, but he shares a great deal with me."

Elizabeth's cheeks warmed, and she looked away. "Does he?"

"Yes." Georgiana paused and then said, "I assume you are wondering whether he told me about his proposal."

Elizabeth drew in a sharp breath. "Yes... yes, I did wonder," she faltered. "I... I have only told two people." She looked back to Georgiana, who was getting up from the bed.

She came over and sat down next to Elizabeth on her bed and took her hand. "He only told me that day we were expecting you and your aunt and uncle to visit." She shook her head. "I believe I may be the only one he has ever told, save perhaps our cousin Richard, but of that I am not certain."

"Did he tell you very much about it?"

"I do not believe he told me all, only that there had been misunderstanding on both of your parts when you refused him."

Elizabeth's stomach swirled in distress at recalling that day, and she cast her eyes down as she fingered the counterpane on her bed. "I do not wish to betray anything he would wish to keep from you, but I will say that on my part, I was not expecting it. I had not the faintest notion that he had such strong feelings for me that would compel him to offer for me." She shook her head. "I misunderstood much of his character, having attributed many things I saw to..." She shook her head and then turned to Georgiana. "He was always standing off by himself. I felt he looked down on those in our neighbourhood."

"I can understand how you would feel that way, because I have seen him exhibit that behaviour. You see, he is... he has..." She paused and shook her head. "Elizabeth, my brother is very guarded, as we both are. He is cautious of allowing people to get close to him because of many who only see him as a prize for what they can get from him."

Elizabeth took a moment before she answered. "I now comprehend what a good man he is and how wrong I was."

Georgiana smiled. "He is a good man, and I was glad when he informed me that while at the bookstore, the two of you seemed to reach an accord."

"We did. We both readily admitted the error of our words and actions." Elizabeth squeezed Georgiana's hand. "We apologized and agreed to put it all behind us." Her heart suddenly lurched at the truth of those words, and she fought back tears that were beginning to fill her eyes. She wondered if she would ever be able to put it all completely behind her. Was she destined to love him forever when he no longer returned that love?

Georgiana stood up and walked back over to her bed. "I may be inclined to view my brother as a perfect gentleman, despite knowing he likely has many faults. I do know that there are many ladies who would be willing to marry him regardless of those faults, only because of who he is and what he has." She pulled back the blankets and crawled into bed. Once settled, she turned back to Elizabeth. "I think the fact that you refused him revealed what superior character you possess; one that he has seldom seen." She smiled. "Good night, Elizabeth."

Elizabeth got up and promptly blew out the candles before her tears could be seen by the young girl. She walked over to her bed and crawled in. "Good night, Georgiana."

As she lay in the darkness, her mind reeled with thoughts of Mr. Darcy, his sister, and Pemberley. When she felt the slightest encouragement that he might still have feelings for her, she would remind herself how her foot injury would be a hindrance to him. She closed her eyes as a tear trailed down her cheek.

"Elizabeth?"

"Yes, Georgiana?"

"I always wanted a sister. I so enjoyed my time with you this evening, and I believe it is the closest thing to having a sister that I will ever experience. Thank you."

Elizabeth's chest constricted at the young girl's words. She was not certain she would be able to utter a single word, but she moistened her lips, swallowed, and said, "Georgiana, I would take you as a sister any day." With that, her tears fell freely.

Chapter 18

Elizabeth slept fitfully through the night but was grateful Georgiana appeared to have slept soundly. When the sunlight began to peer through the window, she decided to wait before rising so as not to waken her guest.

As she lay there, she had no book to read or needlework sampler to work on, so she was left with her thoughts. She wondered what the day would bring. She knew she would see Mr. Darcy when he came with the carriage to return his sister and Mrs. Annesley to their home in London.

Would she have an opportunity to speak with him? Would they have time alone to converse? Would he stay long or leave directly? Would he give her any indication of what his thoughts and feelings might be? Should she just accept what she already knew was likely true?

She must possess a certain something in her air and manner of walking... Miss Bingley's declaration of the traits of an accomplished woman taunted her. Mr. Darcy had agreed with her estimation, even adding more to her long list. She shuddered as he considered how inelegant she must appear to those with a critical eye.

The Bennet household soon grew loud and busy as everyone rose to prepare for the day. Georgiana and Mrs. Annesley would be leaving this morning, and both of Elizabeth's aunts and uncles and their families would be leaving in the early afternoon, so they were preparing for their departure. Poor Hill was frantically scurrying about Longbourn, trying to assist their guests in whatever way she could to assure the comfort of everyone.

Mr. Darcy arrived just as his sister and her companion finished eating breakfast. He visited for a while, and then thanked Mr. and Mrs. Bennet for their hospitality. He stepped outside with his sister and Mrs. Annesley as their belongings were brought out. Elizabeth joined them, taking slow, measured steps, being mindful not to stumble or wince from the pain.

Georgiana and Mrs. Annesley stood off to the side, giving Elizabeth an opportunity to speak to Mr. Darcy. "How did you find the inn, Mr. Darcy?"

He drew in a long breath. "Your description of it was quite accurate, unfortunately, and I did not sleep well at all. I am grateful Georgiana and Mrs. Annesley were not subject to all the vulgar language and commotion that penetrated the paper-thin walls throughout the night."

Elizabeth shook her head. "I am sorry."

"Please do not concern yourself. You did, after all, warn me and offer an alternative. Besides, on the way here, I secured a room at the Meryton Inn, so I hope tonight I will sleep much better."

"You are staying in the neighbourhood?" Her heart soared with hope.

He turned and looked at her for a long moment. "I am, although the length of my stay is not yet decided."

"I see." His eyes conveyed something she could not decipher. Before she could determine its meaning, he asked a question.

"Are your aunts and uncles and their families soon to take their leave?"

"They will likely be on their way shortly."

"Then I should leave so you can spend time with them before their departure. I will ride with the ladies back to the Meryton Inn, and once they are on their way to London, I will attempt to get a little sleep."

"I hope you are successful."

He gave a shrug. "As do I, although I do not normally sleep during the day."

Elizabeth smiled. "I take your meaning, sir. Until my accident, I rarely took naps. Now I find myself falling asleep in the oddest places and at the most unexpected times." She bit her lip. "As you may have noticed when you arrived with Georgiana yesterday."

He gave her an assuring smile. "You most likely needed it."

Elizabeth felt a blush warm her cheeks. She had a difficult time formulating a single intelligent thought when he smiled at her. She thought of her aunt's poem and chuckled. "Apparently I did."

He tilted his head and looked at her as if he were about to say something but remained silent.

Once everything was readied for their departure, Georgiana and Mrs. Annesley approached and again thanked Elizabeth for all she and her family had done to make their stay a pleasant one.

"It was our pleasure. I enjoyed getting to know you, Georgiana."

Georgiana approached Elizabeth and threw her arms around her. As she leaned in, she whispered, "I also want to thank you for showing me what it is like to have a sister. I hope we will meet again soon."

Elizabeth whispered back, "As do I."

The two ladies were helped into the carriage, and as they settled themselves, Darcy turned back to Elizabeth.

"Miss Bennet, I hope you have a good day." He nodded a farewell and then stepped up into the carriage. She stood and watched it until it was out of sight.

~~*

Later that afternoon, after all their guests had taken their leave of Longbourn, Elizabeth, taking her time to be slow and careful, walked outside and sat down on a bench on the east side of the house. The air was warm, but there was a slight breeze that stirred the leaves and flower petals. She glanced towards Oakham Mount, feeling a powerful regret that she could not walk up the trail that led to the top. On such a beautiful day as this, she knew she would have set out directly for it if not for her injury.

She leaned back and closed her eyes and felt the breeze – mingled with the scent of the nearby flowers – waft across her face. She could very easily fall asleep out here.

Her breathing became slower as she considered how grateful she had been for the busyness of the morning after the Darcys left, for it left little time for her to dwell on them. If she thought too much about Mr. Darcy, she would have been hopelessly lost in tears.

"Miss Bennet!"

Elizabeth started at the shrill voice, again being roused from an unplanned nap. She shook her head to rid herself of the drowsiness plaguing her and turned to see Caroline Bingley taking brisk, long strides towards her.

"Good afternoon, Miss Bingley."

Caroline glanced disdainfully about her; then turned back to Elizabeth with an insincere smile. "How are you today, Miss Bennet?" She looked down at Elizabeth's foot. "I am surprised to find you outside. Should you not be resting after your little... incident yesterday?"

"My incident?"

"Your unfortunate stumble at the wedding. What a shame all eyes were upon you."

Elizabeth fisted her hands but was able to return a smile. "I am quite well, and I thank you for your sincere concern for my present wellbeing."

"Mm." Miss Bingley paused and drew in a breath. "I inquired at the door, and they informed me Mr. Darcy and his sister had already left. I had hoped to pay them my respects prior to their return to London."

"Yes, they departed Longbourn this morning." Elizabeth smiled, knowing that while this was the truth, it had confirmed Miss Bingley's misapprehension.

After a long pause, Miss Bingley finally said, "Miss Eliza, I cannot help but caution you not to consider Mr. Darcy's acceptance of your offer to stay at Longbourn as anything more than his feeling compelled to oblige you. He and his sister ought to have stayed at Netherfield. You cannot truly comprehend who he is and what he is accustomed to as his due. Netherfield would have been much more suited to his taste and answered as to what a gentleman of his class expects." She shook her head. "His poor sister had no idea what she was agreeing to when she accepted your invitation!"

"On the contrary, Miss Darcy seemed to enjoy herself very much," Elizabeth said calmly, while on the inside, she was seething.

"Oh, she is far too meek to have said anything disparaging of the inferior accommodations."

Elizabeth lifted a questioning brow. "Meek? I observed her speaking her mind and strongly stating her opinions several times yesterday." She purposely ignored the latter part of Miss Bingley's statement.

Miss Bingley's brows lowered. "Did she? Well, be that as it may, it was still very inappropriate to have them stay at Longbourn!" She pointed her finger at Elizabeth. "I know very well what your motives were in asking them to stay, and while I hate to be the one to cause you disappointment, be assured that Mr. Darcy has the highest expectations for the woman he will one day marry. You heard his strictures on the accomplishments he looks for in a lady, many of which you are obviously lacking."

"My accomplishments – or lack thereof – are known to him. I do not pretend to be anyone I am not, Miss Bingley, and my motive for extending the invitation to stay at Longbourn was out of concern for Miss Darcy. I could not imagine her staying at the inn outside of town."

"A convenient ploy, Miss Bennet, but this will not do! You attempted to use your feminine wiles to draw him in. Consider your lack of style, connections, fortune, and... elegance." She let out a spiteful laugh as she again looked down at Elizabeth's foot. "Consider how he would be viewed with a lady on his arm who limps, stumbles, and cannot dance at a ball."

"If Mr. Darcy were to choose to have me on his arm in spite of those things, I would be honoured, but it is solely up to him." She stood up and took a few measured steps towards Miss Bingley. "I have not used any feminine wiles or arts and allurements or anything else to draw him in. I have always been true to myself around him."

Miss Bingley drew back and laughed. "Ah, yes. Showing up at Netherfield covered in mud just to see your sick sister." She displayed a contemptuous grin. "We certainly observed the true Miss Elizabeth Bennet that day! Oh, the laughter we shared once you left the room."

Elizabeth's jaw tightened. "I am glad to have brought a little levity to your party."

"But consider, Eliza, how you would be censured, slighted, and despised by everyone connected with him. Consider his esteemed family. I know them well and socialize with them on a regular basis. Your alliance would be a disgrace to them; your name would never be mentioned by any of them. For his sake, as well as theirs, you must not entertain any thoughts about securing him."

"Securing him? I fear you do not know Mr. Darcy well, for he is a man who can certainly make up his own mind about his own affairs, including his own alliances. I believe he can readily recognize when a woman is using her arts and allurements in any attempt to entrap him." She tilted her head and arched a brow. "I believe he would run far in the other direction from such a conniving woman." She added silently, *"Even going so far as to spend the night at a disreputable inn outside of town!"*

"But would he ever step foot in Cheapside? I doubt he would wish to visit your aunt and uncle there, given your uncle's involvement in trade." She sent Elizabeth a challenging look.

"Miss Bingley, you have seriously misjudged Mr. Darcy's character as well as greatly mistaken mine. I believe you have said quite enough, Madam, and since you so easily discovered me out here, I believe you can also find your way back to your carriage."

"I beg your pardon. We are sisters now." replied Miss Bingley with a false smile. "Excuse my interference – it was kindly meant." She turned with a huff and began to walk away.

"Miss Bingley," Elizabeth called out, halting the woman. "One more thing, if you please. I would have you know that Mr. Darcy did not stay here last night." Elizabeth smiled at Miss Bingley's dropped jaw. "I extended the invitation solely to Miss Darcy and her companion, believing they should not stay the night at the inn. We had room enough to accommodate the women, but not enough to offer the same to Mr. Darcy."

Miss Bingley looked intently at Elizabeth, as if attempting to determine the significance of this intelligence. Soon a smile of relief came upon her face. It was apparent she was pleased with this information. "Oh, I see." Her lips curled in a sneer. "Good day, Miss Bennet."

Elizabeth watched her disappear around the house and without thinking, she stamped her injured foot hard on the ground. She let out a cry and bent over in pain.

She slowly straightened, turned around, and found herself face to face with Mr. Darcy, who was walking towards her from behind a hedgerow.

Chapter 19

Elizabeth drew back in surprise. "Mr. Darcy!"

He clasped his fingers and shook his head as he came near to her. "Pray, forgive me. I did not wish to startle you."

"How long have you been standing there?"

His mouth twisted in a frown. "Long enough to have heard Miss Bingley's contemptible and... accusatory attack."

Elizabeth tilted her head and with a sly smile asked, "Do you make a habit of eavesdropping?"

He pressed his lips together. "As a matter of fact, I do not. I was not able to hear everything that was said, Miss Bennet, save for the times Miss Bingley raised her voice." He gave her a smile. "From your apparent calm manner and tone of voice and Miss Bingley's increased look of frustration, I determined you were doing quite well and needed no help from me." He lowered his brows. "It was very wrong of her to say such things."

"I believe she was upset. I finally decided I would correct her misapprehension that you stayed here last night." She gave a slight shrug. "I knew she would find out eventually, and as we are now sisters, I did not wish for her to wonder what my motives might be for keeping the truth from her."

"Still, she ought not have said such things about me... and more particularly, about you."

Elizabeth looked away and drew in a long breath, her shoulders rising and then falling as she let it out. "Perhaps, but I fear she was... correct, Mr. Darcy." Elizabeth looked down at her fingers, which she was knitting together. "As I walked through Pemberley last summer, I could not help but think of the grand balls and parties that one would have there – that the Mistress of Pemberley would host." She opened her hands, waving them towards her foot. "I cannot dance; I can barely even walk." She shook away tears that began to pool in her eyes. "I have no unrealistic hopes about my condition, Mr. Darcy. It is likely not to improve any more than it has." She turned to look at him. "And I have no unrealistic expectations about..." She shook her head. "Well, that which Miss Bingley believes prompted the offer I extended to your sister to stay at Longbourn."

"Is that truly what you believe?"

"How can I not?" She gave a slight shrug.

Darcy began tapping his legs with his hands. He then rubbed his jaw as he pondered her words.

"Come, let us sit," he said as he brought her over to the bench.

"Thank you."

When they sat on the bench, Elizabeth was very much aware of his closeness to her.

He was silent for a moment, and then said, "I fear, Miss Bennet..." He began slowly, his voice a husky whisper, "I fear that you are under a misapprehension, and just as you corrected Miss Bingley's, I feel it is necessary for me to correct yours."

"My misapprehension? And what might that be?"

"You have an inaccurate view of the type of woman I want as my wife." He leaned forward and rested his arms on his legs, clasping his hands.

Elizabeth sent him a sideways glance, tilting her head. "In what way, sir?"

"I am not looking for a woman to wed merely to be the Mistress of Pemberley." He leaned back, his broad shoulder touching hers. "Would this be a correct assumption of yours?"

She felt the same dizzying shudder that she had felt yesterday when he sat next to her. She could barely concentrate on anything else with him so near, let alone how to answer him. After a moment, she asked, "Would not your wife *be* the Mistress of Pemberley?"

"Oh, indeed! But the woman I am looking to wed, must first and foremost..." He paused, and in a whisper said, "She must first be my wife, one whom I ardently love and admire."

Elizabeth felt barely able to breathe. He had explicitly expressed his ardent love and admiration for her when he began his proposal a little over a year ago. His gaze alone was enough to unsettle her and make her forget her ailment.

"But Mr. Darcy..."

He put up a hand to stay her. "You seem to believe that my wife... the Mistress of Pemberley... must be without defect because you believe... wrongly, I might add... that I am without defect."

She shook her head. "Mr. Darcy, I told you already how wrongly I had judged you. I no longer consider your actions and behaviour in Hertfordshire to have been flawed."

He smiled. "Well, I do appreciate that, but that is not the subject I address at this moment."

Elizabeth's brows lowered. "I fear I do not understand, then."

"There is something else... something about me very few people know."

She sent him a questioning glance. "Of what do you speak?"

"Lizzy!" Both Darcy and Elizabeth turned to see Kitty running towards them.

"Oh!" Kitty stopped. "I did not know Mr. Darcy was here."

"What is it, Kitty?" Elizabeth asked in frustration.

"Mr. Arnold has arrived. He is now in the parlour."

Elizabeth lifted her hands in question. "Why are you coming out here to tell me? Did he ask for me?"

Kitty shook her head. "I do not know, for I have not yet seen him. He is in with Mother, Lydia, and Mary."

Elizabeth chuckled. "Kitty, if I were you, I would return to the parlour directly. Mr. Arnold is likely to be subject to a complete account of Mother's vexations and Mary's discourse from one of Fordyce's sermons. And I cannot imagine what Lydia might contribute to the conversation."

A look of concern passed over Kitty's face. "But what am I to talk with him about?"

Elizabeth sent her a stern glance, touched with a slight smile. "You are certainly capable of carrying on a sensible conversation."

"But what shall we discuss? We already talked of Cowper's poetry."

Elizabeth reached for her sister's hand. "Begin by asking him how he is, how his aunt and uncle are, and then see where the conversation goes from there. He might even bring up a topic of conversation himself."

Kitty clenched her fists and brought them to her side. "All right, but I would much prefer it if you were there."

Elizabeth waved her off. "You will do admirably."

Kitty looked at the house and then back to them. "All right, but this is not as easy for me as it is for you." She turned and walked away.

They watched her retreating figure, and Elizabeth said softly, "I hope she will prove me right."

"Would you prefer... to join her and visit with Mr. Arnold?"

Elizabeth concealed the smile that threatened to appear at the look of trepidation on Mr. Darcy's face. Did he think she would say she would prefer to be with Mr. Arnold? Did he hope she would say no?

"Assuredly not! I have been trying to encourage her to grow in confidence and learn the art of conversing – especially with a young gentleman." She turned back to look at Kitty, as she disappeared around the house. "No, I would much prefer to remain here."

Darcy noticeably relaxed and let out a soft breath.

She looked at him with a mischievous smile. "Besides, you were about to confess a glaring defect of yours, and I am eager to discover its nature!"

"I do not believe I said it was glaring." He met her smile with one of his own and looked about the grounds. "But before I do so, I should like to be certain there are no listening ears nearby."

Elizabeth laughed. "Much like yours?"

Darcy nodded with a guilty smile. "I would very much like to walk up Oakham Mount."

Elizabeth drew back aghast. "Up Oakham Mount?" She shook her head and gestured towards her foot. "I cannot. You know I would not be able to manage it, as much as I would like to."

He smiled at her. "I thought as much. Do you think, however, that you would be able to walk to the front of the house?" He lifted a brow.

"The front? I think so."

Darcy stood and reached out for her hand, gently pulling her up. At his touch, Elizabeth felt a wavy of dizziness pass through her and a warmth flooded her cheeks. He tucked her arm through his, and they began to walk.

She glanced down at his hand and then took it in her free hand, opening it and turning it around, as if to inspect it. She silently admired his long fingers and trimmed and clean fingernails.

He let out a soft groan. "Miss Bennet, pray what are you doing?"

"Just inspecting for any defect. You do have four fingers and a thumb," she said, looking up with a smile.

He held up his other hand. "And this one does, as well."

She tilted her head. "Indeed. Perhaps your defect is that you are missing your big toe on both feet."

He grew serious. "I have all my toes. Come. I will tell you shortly."

They walked slowly, Elizabeth did her best to walk as elegantly as possible and not stumble. She knew she had not the air and manner of walking that Miss Bingley had spoken about.

Mr. Darcy brought her to the front of the house where a horse was tethered. They walked up to it.

"What is this?" she asked.

"A horse," he answered matter-of-factly.

"Yes, I can see that, but..."

"I believe her name is Princess. She is Bingley's gentlest and most sure-footed mare." Without saying another word, he put his strong hands about Elizabeth's small waist and lifted her up, placing her side-saddle on the horse.

"What are you doing?"

"We are going to go up Oakham Mount!"

Elizabeth began to laugh. "I have never in my life ridden a horse up the hill. You cannot be serious."

"I have never been more serious in my life."

"I really do not know about this," Elizabeth said as Darcy untethered the horse and began to lead it – and her – away.

He turned back. "Do you wish to learn about my defect or not?"

Elizabeth could not help but chuckle. "Onward, then, sir. I suppose I am at your mercy."

He smiled and gazed intently at her. "I do believe I like that thought."

She felt her cheeks warm again, but this time she did not care if he noticed.

Chapter 20

Elizabeth and Darcy were silent as they made the ascent up Oakham Mount. He led in front when the path was narrow, and when it widened, he walked at Elizabeth's side. Halfway up the hill, they came to an overlook, and Darcy stopped to wrap the reins about a tree limb. He stepped back and reached up, bringing Elizabeth off the horse, his hands lingering briefly about her waist as he gently set her down.

"Before I confess my defect to you, come look at the view. I have been up here several times, and I believe this is my favourite place to view the landscape below." A smile touched his lips as he brought her to the edge of the path overlooking the countryside.

"It is my favourite, as well," Elizabeth said, returning his smile. "It is especially beautiful in autumn, when the trees are vibrant oranges and reds."

"Yes, I remember well. When I was here with Bingley that autumn, I frequently came up here when I needed to think."

Elizabeth clasped her hands and looked down as she reflected back on a year and a half ago when the two men had come into their neighbourhood.

"There were times I needed to get away from..." He looked down in the direction of Netherfield. "...a certain lady who refused to leave me alone."

Elizabeth chuckled and softly said, "Yes, I can imagine." She let out a sigh. "With the onset of winter, going to London, and then my accident, I have not been up here for at least five months. I have missed it." She then turned to him. "Thank you for bringing me."

"You are welcome. I hoped you would enjoy it."

They looked silently for a few moments out across the colourful landscape below.

"The blossoms are especially abundant right now." She nodded towards their left. "Mr. Agnew will likely have a large crop of apples later this year."

"If the frigid temperatures had come through even a few days later, it could have wiped out any hope of a good crop."

Elizabeth looked down at her foot. "And yet, if the frigid temperatures had come through a few days later, perhaps I would not have fallen and would still be able to walk up here on my own two feet."

She lifted her eyes and saw he was looking at her. They stared at each other a few moments in silence. Elizabeth felt a small ray of hope that what she saw in his eyes was the same depth of love he once felt for her – and that she now felt for him. She could not be certain, however, and did not want to risk letting her heart hope. She abruptly turned away.

He broke the silence. "Miss Bennet, are you ready to hear what I have to say?"

It took Elizabeth a moment to realize what he was talking about. "Oh, your defect! Of course, I am most curious to hear what trait you possess that you consider to be a defect." She was grateful to be able to laugh, but quickly realized Mr. Darcy's demeanour was solemn.

Darcy looked up and away. When he looked back at her, his expression was one of pain but also determination. "Not many people are aware of this. Truly, only my closest family knows."

Elizabeth felt her insides roil as she comprehended the anguish this must be causing him. She remained silent but gave her head a nod for him to continue.

"Miss Bennet, when I was a child, it was determined that I had a slight hearing defect. My left ear is worse than my right, but it is severe enough to cause me great difficulty in certain situations."

Elizabeth's jaw dropped, and she shook her head. "Truly? I never perceived your having any hearing impairment."

He clasped his hands behind his back and began to pace, occasionally glancing over to her. "I have learned to compensate, but there are certain situations where I find it problematic." He raised his brows. "At a ball, for instance. Or a party. When I am in a group of people and there are many raised voices, it is particularly difficult to follow a conversation, especially when there is a great deal of other noise, as well."

Comprehension flooded her as she thought back to his behaviour when he first came to Hertfordshire. "Is that why you often stood by yourself? I assumed it was because you did not wish to associate with those in our neighbourhood."

His eyes closed, and he pressed his lips together. "It has been easier to allow that to be the assumption."

"I cannot imagine how difficult that must be." She looked down and shook her head. She suddenly lifted her eyes. "But our dance at the Netherfield Ball. It seems you were quite capable of carrying on a conversation with me without difficulty. The music was playing, other couples were conversing, and we were not always close."

He began to rub his hands together. "I was doing everything in my power to capture each word you said, either by turning my head so my better ear faced you or by watching you so I could read your lips as you spoke."

Elizabeth's eyes widened, and her jaw dropped. "You are able to read people's lips and know what they are saying?"

"To an extent."

Elizabeth's eyes twinkled with mischief, and she silently mouthed the words, "What am is saying now?"

"What am I saying now?" He lifted a brow to ascertain whether he was correct.

"Indeed." She suddenly frowned. "But sir, how often did you read my lips when you were not within hearing distance of my conversation?"

Darcy sent her a teasing glance. "Enough times to know your true opinion of Miss Bingley."

Elizabeth let out a brief chuckle, but then lowered her brows. "Oh dear, I imagine you have probably learned to use that special ability to your advantage!"

"One might think that true, but unfortunately in your case, I did not come away with any insightful intelligence on how you felt about me that would have assisted me a year ago."

Elizabeth felt a wave of regret and looked away. "I am so sorry..."

Darcy put a finger up to her lips. "We have both already confessed our shortcomings and forgiven each other. All is forgotten."

Elizabeth trembled when he drew his finger away. Her face suddenly lit up. "You told me at Rosings that you were unable to catch someone's tone of conversation or appear interested in their concerns. Is this due to your being unable to hear things clearly?"

"I hoped you might understand, but I did not wish to make my deafness known to all that were there."

"Does your aunt not know?"

"Oh, she most certainly knows, as well as Anne, the Colonel and his family, and of course, Georgiana. There are a few others who know. My aunt never speaks of it to anyone but me, and that is solely to reinforce how perfect Anne and I are for each other. With Anne's frail condition and my deafness, she often claimed a union between us was meant to be." He let out a long breath. "She often made the claim that no other lady of such excellent breeding and fortune would accept me."

"I see." Elizabeth suddenly drew back. "So, you were forced to settle for a lady with little breeding, poor connections, and no fortune! Mr. Darcy, pray tell me, was that your motivation in offering for me?"

A look of horror crossed Darcy's face. "Pray, do not think for a moment that was the reason! There is nothing further from the truth!"

Elizabeth smiled, and her eyes twinkled. "Calm yourself, Mr. Darcy. Do you not know I was teasing you?"

He reached for her hand. "Miss Bennet, I want to assure you, teasing or not, that I offered for you because I found in you someone I enjoyed being with, whom I had grown to love. I loved how honest you were with me. You were willing to express opinions that did not merely agree with mine. You were willing to challenge me and debate me, and you exhibited an intelligence and liveliness that I was irresistibly drawn to." He looked down at her hand. "I had fallen in love with you, Elizabeth, and wanted nothing more than to live out my years with you. *That* was my motivation for offering for you."

Elizabeth's mouth went dry, and she swallowed hard. "And then I refused you."

Darcy brought her hand up, covering it with his other hand. "At first, I was angry and confused, and I felt the world had turned upside down on me. But as time went on, I came to realize just how much your refusal served to reinforce my feelings for you." He paused and looked up at her intently. "What you did exhibited a great depth to your character."

"My refusal did that?"

"When I asked you to become my wife, I was offering to you everything that was mine, and yet you were willing to walk away from it all. I realized the principles that guided your refusal were stronger than any desire you had for what came with my name."

"I see." They remained silent for a moment, and then Elizabeth said, "One more question, if you please."

Darcy nodded for her to continue.

"If I had accepted your offer, exactly *when* would you have informed me of your defect?" She sent him a questioning look accompanied with a sly smile. "On our wedding night, perhaps?"

Darcy pressed his lips together in thought. "I confess it was not on my mind that day, but I assure you, I would have told you *before* our wedding night." He gave her a pointed glance.

Elizabeth pressed her other hand over his, prompting Darcy to look down and study it. When he looked back at her beautiful face, his eyes were filled with tenderness. "You see, Miss Bennet, whether or not you can dance means nothing to me. If in time your foot heals, I would be delighted to have you accompany me to a ball, join me on the dance floor, or walk by my side about the grounds of Longbourn or... Pemberley, because, Elizabeth, you are the one I ardently love and admire." He removed his hands from between hers and enclosed them between his, squeezing them tightly. He looked at her intently. "Still."

Elizabeth felt great euphoria at Mr. Darcy's pronouncement. *He still loves me, and my injury matters not to him!*

She looked down at their hands and noticed his thumb tracing circles on the back of her wrist. That slight touch mesmerized her, and she lifted her eyes to him.

She began to speak slowly. "Mr. Darcy, when I regained my memory of what happened that day in London, one of the first things I remembered was walking out of the bookstore and realizing that... that I had come to love you." She spoke softly, yet with a heartfelt intensity. "I love you."

Darcy cupped her chin with his hand and drew close to her. In a husky whisper, he said, "Elizabeth, you have no idea how I have longed to hear you speak those three little words." He leaned forward, pressing his lips to hers.

Elizabeth's eyes widened at the touch of his lips, and at length, she closed them when he wrapped his arms about her. She was certain that if he had not been holding her, she would have crumpled to the ground, and not owing to her injured foot.

It was a few moments before he pulled away. "Elizabeth, pray forgive me. I hope you do not consider my kiss bold, improper, or imprudent." He brought his hands up and fingered a loose lock of her hair.

She gently wrapped her fingers about his and brought them to her lips, kissing them. She glanced up at him. "Does this answer your question?"

"It does," he replied. Shaking his head, he added, "The journey we have taken to get to this place has been too long."

She gave him a reassuring smile. "It has certainly been a long... and an *interesting* journey."

"But one that we needed to take..." He swallowed hard. "...even with all the obstacles along the way. It is a journey that – I hope – will continue." He reached for her hand. "Elizabeth, my greatest desire is to continue this journey with you by my side." He paused and slipped down on one knee. "Would you do me the honour of becoming my wife? You are the one I have ardently loved and admired for the past year and a half, and I will spend my whole life continuing in that love."

He studied her face intently, waiting for her answer.

Elizabeth's heart soared, and she felt she could barely breathe. "I would be honoured to accept your offer of marriage, Fitzwilliam."

She was rewarded with a broad smile. He took her in his arms and unapologetically kissed her again, this time with more fervour.

He did not seem at all inclined to cease.

When he finally pulled away, he looked at her and asked, "Shall we go inform your family? I would like to get your father's permission directly."

"Oh, dear!" Elizabeth cried. "This will not do!"

"What? Do you not think your father will consent to our marrying?"

"Oh, I believe he will, but Jane is not here! I do not have Jane to tell!"

"But you have three sisters who *are* here... as well as your mother," he added with a single raised brow.

Elizabeth laughed. "I think we both know how *my mother* will take the news, but how I wish I could tell Jane." She let out a long sigh and then smiled. "Do you think perhaps I ought to share the news with Miss Bingley?" She tilted her head and smiled.

"Now, that would certainly prove to be interesting!" He let out a chuckle. "I think we can both imagine how *Miss Bingley* will take the news! Remind me not to go anywhere near Netherfield in the next month!"

Chapter 21

Darcy and Elizabeth took their time descending Oakham Mount. This time, when the path was wide, he walked along Elizabeth's side with his hand resting on her back. They exchanged smiles, laughter, and many endearing sentiments to each other. When the path was narrow and Darcy was forced to walk in front, he often turned back to make certain she was doing well.

He commented on how lovely she looked with the sun's brilliant highlights upon her dark hair, how the fresh air caused a glow on her face, and that her eyes, which he had always considered fine, now captivated him with their sparkle.

Elizabeth, not to be outdone, commented on how the breeze stirred his dark curly hair, how his face glowed with the healthy aftermath of a long walk, and how his demeanour of joy seemed to accentuate his dimples, making him even more handsome and irresistible to her. He appeared uneasy with the compliments but smiled nonetheless, revealing those rarely seen dimples again. During this exchange he was walking by her side, and she reached over and playfully tousled the curls she had just praised. When she had finished, she dropped her hand to his neck, letting it rest there briefly.

When she withdrew her hand, Darcy snatched it and brought it to his lips. "You delight in tormenting me, Elizabeth!" He proceeded to kiss each of her fingers.

She sent him a stern glance. "I have done nothing you have not done!" She gave her head a quick shake to settle the matter.

The path to Longbourn brought them to the back of the home, and Darcy lifted Elizabeth down from the horse and carried her to the bench on which she had been sitting earlier.

"So, we are back to where it all began," she said with a smile.

"I beg to disagree, Elizabeth." He touched her nose with his finger. "It all began that night at the Meryton Assembly."

"On the contrary, my dearest Fitzwilliam! You insulted me with your unkind remark and left me with no cordial feelings for you!"

He wrapped his arms about her. "That remark was not intended for your ears, and it was said merely to serve as a warning to myself that I found you exceedingly beautiful."

She laughed. "You certainly have a way of *not* making a good first impression with all the ladies."

"And you, Elizabeth, are definitely *not* all the ladies."

When he pulled her close and kissed her again, Elizabeth was grateful for the hedgerow that separated them from the house. She placed her hands lightly against his chest and revelled in the strong beating of his heart against her fingers.

He drew back and whispered, "I love you more than words can say, Elizabeth."

She smiled and stroked his cheek. "I do not need your words, Fitzwilliam. I can see it on your face and feel it in your touch."

He lightly kissed her lips again, and when he pulled away, they both sensed someone nearby.

They turned and saw Miss Bingley standing there.

"Miss Bingley!" they both exclaimed.

The flustered woman stood gaping at them. Her face was red with rage, and the only sound she seemed capable of making was a slight squeak.

"What are you doing here?" Elizabeth asked, attempting to gain her composure. "Did you forget something?"

The woman walked towards them slowly, sending accusatory glances at the couple. "I had seen Charles' horse here when I left earlier, and when I inquired at Netherfield, I was told Mr. Darcy left his horse there and had taken Princess. I came back to see if he was still here." She began to shake her finger at the two of them. "Not only do I find he is here, but find he is in... was in... What I just witnessed was... was... abhorrent! I have never witnessed such a display of impropriety!" She looked at Mr. Darcy. "It was very wrong, but I am certain Miss Bennet enticed you into her arms with her arts and allurements. You made a mistake, and it will all be forgotten. I shall not mention it to anyone, lest it becomes known you compromised her and are forced to wed her!" She shook her head wildly. "I shall not be the one who forces such an unequal and dreadful marriage upon you!"

Elizabeth began, "Miss Bingley, I fear you are mistaken and do not understand..."

Miss Bingley lifted her chin and sneered. "I most certainly do understand the ways of the world and how a desperate woman employs tactics that undermine the common sense of a gentleman!"

Elizabeth's eyes widened. "I used no arts or allurements, and most certainly am not a desperate woman!"

Darcy stepped forward. "Miss Bingley, what you came upon was a most natural outcome of my most fervent love for Elizabeth."

"Love? Elizabeth? That cannot be!"

"I would have you know..." Darcy began, but Elizabeth raised her hand to stop him.

"Miss Bingley, it is very convenient that you came upon us just now! I was earlier saying to Mr. Darcy that I wished Jane were here to share some wonderful news with her. And then I thought... and I told this to Mr. Darcy... that perhaps I could confide in you!" She leaned in with a smile.

"What... whatever do you mean?" Miss Bingley stammered.

Elizabeth looked over to Mr. Darcy, who wore a wide smile on his face. He gave a nod for her to continue.

"Well, as I said, it is wonderful! Mr. Darcy has made me an offer of marriage, and I accepted! We are now engaged!"

Miss Bingley emitted another squeak, and her mouth twitched uncontrollably.

Elizabeth walked over to her and took her hand. "So, you see, Caroline... May I call you Caroline as we are now sisters? You may be the first to congratulate us!"

Miss Bingley drew herself erect, straightened her shoulders, and gave her head a shake as she glared at Mr. Darcy. Turning back to Elizabeth, she sputtered, "I offer the two of you... great... joy." She practically spit out the last word, and her lips spread in what may have been an attempt to smile. Saying no more, she turned and walked away.

When she disappeared around the front of the house, Elizabeth pressed her fingers to her lips. She turned to Mr. Darcy. "Was I terribly unkind just now?"

Darcy laughed. "You were most congenial, Elizabeth, but I can guarantee that Miss Bingley will not be the same for quite some time. I would not have been so kind to her."

"Oh, dear. How I feel sorry for Jane when she and Charles return to Netherfield. If Caroline is still there, it will likely prove to be most unpleasant!!"

"As I have felt sorry for Bingley all the years I have known him!"

They shared a laugh, and then Darcy said, "As soon as I see that Miss Bingley has left, I will go directly to see your father."

"Yes, please do!" Elizabeth exclaimed. "Before anyone else comes along and finds us together, assuming the worst."

"But first..." He leaned down and kissed her again.

He drew back, and when they saw Miss Bingley's carriage depart, they walked around to the front of the house. Elizabeth's hand was tucked in Mr. Darcy's arm, and they walked close, smiling and laughing. As they took the steps up to the door, it was opened by Hill, and Mr. Arnold stepped out. He greeted the two with a look of surprise.

"Mr. Darcy! Miss Bennet!"

"Mr. Arnold," Darcy greeted him back.

"Mr. Arnold... did you have a pleasant visit?" Elizabeth asked.

"I did, thank you." He looked back and forth at the couple facing him.

Elizabeth looked at Hill, who remained at the door. "Hill, would you please take Mr. Darcy to Father's study? He wishes to see him."

The woman nodded, and Darcy excused himself.

Elizabeth turned back to Mr. Arnold, and knew by the questioning look on his face, she must explain. "You may wonder..."

Mr. Arnold laughed. "Oh, I do not wonder. I have readily seen something between you and Mr. Darcy from that first day he visited Longbourn."

Elizabeth softly chuckled. "You saw it with Jane and Charles, and you recognized the same thing between Mr. Darcy and me? You are truly astute! For at that time, I was not aware there was anything between us."

"I admit there was something different, which I have been unable to discern."

Elizabeth let out a long sigh. "It is a long, complicated story, which I may – or may not – tell you one day."

"I understand, but pray, there is one thing you can tell me."

"Yes?"

"Is there an esteemed gentleman about to appear who will attach Kitty's affections? I am about to give up on the Bennet ladies."

Elizabeth's clasped her hands together. "But are your affections attached to her, Mr. Arnold? If they are, I would be delighted!"

"She is a sweet girl, and I have enjoyed getting to know her."

"I am so pleased to hear that!" She smiled at him. "And no, I know of no gentleman, esteemed or otherwise, who might suddenly appear."

"That is reassuring, indeed."

"But then, if one does show up, there is always Lydia." She gave him a teasing smile.

"Yes, well, Lydia is too young and a bit too flirtatious for me." He let out a breathy laugh. "She quickly lost any interest in me when she realized that I did not respond to her flirtatious ways."

"True." Elizabeth tilted her head and pinched her brows. "But tell me, Mr. Arnold, what is it about the Bennet daughters that caught your attention? For there are certainly other ladies in the neighbourhood and, of course, in all of England. If I may be so bold as to ask, why does it seem you have been intent on singling one of us out?" She laughed. "Not that I mind, of course."

He chuckled. "My aunt said you would be the one who would ask that."

"Your aunt said that?"

He drew in a long breath. "Miss Bennet, are you well-acquainted with my aunt?"

"Most certainly! I always enjoy seeing her at dinner parties or the balls and dances. She has always taken an interest in us."

He bit his lips and then asked, "Do you know why?"

"No, I simply assumed she was very friendly."

"Well, that she is, but what you may not know and might not remember, is that she was of use to your mother after you and your sisters were born."

Elizabeth pinched her brows and looked off in thought. "I do not remember that at all."

"Apparently when your older sister was born, my aunt would stop by occasionally to give your mother an opportunity to rest. When you were born less than two years later, she came more often, and with each successive daughter, your mother seemed to be in greater need of her assistance."

Elizabeth slowly shook her head. "I had no idea."

"Having no children of her own, she grew very fond of all of you, almost viewing you and your sisters as the children she never had."

"I see," Elizabeth said wistfully. She suddenly looked back at Mr. Arnold. "And what does this have to do with you?"

He smiled. "Well, I have grown up hearing all about the Bennet girls... and now ladies. She knew each of you so well and described each of you quite accurately. When I was younger, I was not particularly interested, but in time, I became curious about the five of you."

"So, she accurately described us?" Elizabeth tilted her head. "What did she have to say about us?"

He laughed. "She always said that Miss Bennet... that is, Mrs. Bingley, was the prettiest and sweetest, and that she did not have a mean bone in her body."

"That is certainly Jane." She tilted her head. "And what about me?"

"She said you were pretty, quite intelligent, lively, and..." He paused.

"Oh, dear." She let out a laugh. "What was the reason for that pause?"

"She said you had a little streak of independence... but not in a bad way."

"Well, I am grateful for that!"

"She described Miss Mary as being pretty, but she seemed to

prefer to keep herself as plain looking as she could, that she spent her time reading Fordyce's sermons and would likely marry a parson."

"Correct."

"Now, Miss Kitty, she described as young and pretty, but very impressionable. She said she often feared she was following in the footsteps of the *wrong* sister."

"That wrong sister being Lydia."

"Yes. She told me that Miss Lydia was shockingly flirtatious and if she had been her own daughter, she would have put a stop to her inappropriate behaviour."

"So, in a sense, you came to know us ahead of time through her."

He nodded as he rubbed his jaw. "My aunt and uncle recently informed me that I was to become the heir of their estate." He gave a shrug. "It needs repair, and there is much work that must be done to it. I do not have a great fortune, and I thought if I could offer a home with the potential of a future prospect to a young lady in the neighbourhood, she might be willing to overlook my current circumstances to be able to remain close to her family."

Elizabeth was silent as she comprehended this.

"I assure you, Miss Bennet, that my aunt did not insist I marry one of the Bennet daughters as a prerequisite for receiving the inheritance, but I decided I would see for myself if one of you might be as captivating as my aunt described you."

"I see," Elizabeth said, pondering. "But Mr. Arnold, I would not wish for Kitty to feel as though you are settling for her. She truly deserves to be loved for who she is."

"I understand and completely agree. I believe she is someone I can grow to love."

Elizabeth lifted her brows. "Well, Mr. Arnold, just be aware that Kitty has only recently begun exhibiting signs of maturing. She is just turned eighteen and is still learning how to act and speak like a lady." She smiled. "I hope you will be patient with her." She tilted her head.

"Indeed, I shall!" He gave a quick bow of his head. "I must take my leave now, Miss Bennet, but first, if you please, may I ask a question?"

Elizabeth inclined her head. "Certainly."

"Was Mr. Darcy going to your father to gain his permission to marry you?"

Elizabeth smiled and nodded. "He was."

"Good. I wish you both much happiness."

"Thank you, Mr. Arnold. I hope you will come back soon."

"Oh, I do intend to."

He turned to walk away, but Elizabeth called out to him. "Mr. Arnold, one more thing, if you please."

"Certainly."

"Did your aunt inform you of Mr. Bingley's earlier attachment to Jane?"

Mr. Arnold looked awkwardly at the ground. "Indeed, she did. She told me that everyone believed Mr. Bingley would be offering for her, but he then disappeared." He chuckled. "She also told me that she thought Mr. Darcy was quite enamoured with you, although others in the neighbourhood did not agree."

Elizabeth laughed. "When you said you noticed something between Jane and Charles, and Mr. Darcy and me, was it based on what your aunt had told you?"

"I confess it influenced how I saw you two couples interact, but I could readily see something."

"I believe you and your aunt have the unique ability to sketch someone's character. I hope it serves you well with Kitty."

"Thank you!" he said with a broad smile. "I hope it does, as well!"

She watched him walk away, and then turned to enter the house. "What an extraordinary day this has been." She opened the door but paused before entering. "I wonder how Mother will react to the most extraordinary news I am about to tell her!"

~~*

Mr. and Mrs. Bennet reacted as differently as could be imagined to the news of their daughter marrying Fitzwilliam Darcy. Mr. Bennet was unsure how this ever came about; Mrs. Bennet knew from the beginning that Mr. Darcy would marry one of her daughters. Mr. Bennet was quiet and reflective; Mrs. Bennet's wails and excited flutterings brought the two youngest daughters scrambling down the stairs to see what the matter could be. Mr. Bennet thought of losing his favourite daughter; Mrs. Bennet thought only of a second daughter marrying exceedingly well. Mr. Bennet gave his permission after a thorough questioning; Mrs. Bennet's approval was bestowed immediately, for he was such a wealthy, prominent gentleman.

Even though Mr. Darcy could readily obtain a special license to marry, they determined they would wait, marrying a few weeks after Charles and Jane returned from their wedding journey. The couple would be gone at least two weeks, so they chose a date a month away. Announcements were written up for the newspapers, the banns were prepared to be read, and Mr. Darcy penned a letter to Lady Catherine. He knew that anything he had ever done in the past that had upset her would pale in comparison to this. He believed Anne would understand but doubted his aunt would. It was likely she would never allow herself to give Elizabeth her due as Darcy's wife and the mistress of Pemberley.

Chapter 22

Fitzwilliam Darcy stood at the front of Longbourn Chapel next to his good friend, Charles Bingley. He shifted his weight from one foot to the other as he watched and anxiously waited for the first glimpse of his bride. He could hardly believe that the day he had been dreaming of for so long was finally here.

His friend leaned over to whisper, "Do you realize that just a little over a month ago, I was waiting for my angel to appear? Now I do the same, only under much different circumstances!" He let out a soft chuckle. "I had no idea that I would shortly be standing at your side, about to become your brother!" He shook his head. "Why is it you never mentioned your admiration for Elizabeth? My dearest Jane tried to explain it to me several times, but I still do not fully comprehend."

Darcy drew in a long breath and let it out slowly. "It is rather complicated, Bingley." He fingered his neck cloth. Despite the coolness of the morning, he felt warm and uncomfortable inside the church.

Bingley shook his head. "And I thought it was complicated between Jane and me."

Darcy let out a conceding grunt as he looked out at the crowd. There were both familiar and unfamiliar faces looking back at him, but there were several people conspicuously absent. Lady Catherine and her daughter Anne had not come. He had not expected they would; she had written a scathing letter to him after he informed her of his upcoming marriage. She denounced him, threatened him, and begged him to come to his senses. It was forever her way to be obstinate, he had known, and after he and Elizabeth had been wed a few months, he would write to her again and seek a reconciliation. He believed that his aunt had been fond of Elizabeth when they had formerly met at Rosings, and he knew that her animosity was due solely to his destroying her closely held hopes and dreams of his marrying her daughter. He hoped Anne would warmly welcome Elizabeth into the family.

He noticed that Sir William Lucas and his wife and family were there, but their daughter, Charlotte, and her husband, Mr. Collins, were not. It was likely due to his aunt being firmly against the marriage.

Finally, Caroline Bingley was not present. She and the Hursts had been in London, and when the Hursts returned for the wedding, Caroline sent a message saying she regretted that she had taken ill and could not attend the ceremony. Darcy recognized this had merely been an excuse, and in truth, he did not care.

His cousin, Colonel Fitzwilliam was there with his family. Richard had met Elizabeth when they were in Kent, and his cousin had reassured his family that she was a superior woman and one of whom they would approve. He was grateful that in meeting Elizabeth the previous evening, they had been cordial and gracious to her and her family.

Bingley suddenly gasped as Jane began to walk down the aisle. "Tell me, Darcy, is she not an angel?"

Darcy chuckled, for it was apparent his friend had not lost his admiration for his bride. But he barely noticed Jane, for he was waiting for the woman who had captured his heart to step out.

And he waited. In those few moments, an irrational fear began to rise that she would not appear. He feared he would be tormented again, as he had been that day when she did not come to his town home. He wondered if perhaps she had changed her mind, as had been his thought that day.

Fortunately, it was but a moment later she stepped out on her father's arm. He breathed a loud sigh of relief and admiration, chiding himself inwardly for such a foolish notion. As he gazed at her, he fought the urge to go to her. She was stunning, from her dark, glistening hair, to her sparkling eyes, and to her radiant smile, which was directed at him. He did not think he had ever seen her look more lovely.

Mr. Bennet and his favourite daughter took slow, careful steps as they walked down the aisle, and he could tell she was holding on as tightly to her father as he was to her. He knew that today, his and Elizabeth's wedding day, was the day that Elizabeth wished most not to stumble. He was well aware that her injured foot gave her pain with each cautious step she placed on it. It deeply grieved him that he could not rid her of such suffering, and he felt a depth of love for her that surpassed anything he could have ever imagined existing.

At last, she was by his side, and as they turned to face the clergyman, all Darcy could think was that when they again turned around to face their friends and family, Elizabeth Bennet would be Elizabeth Darcy, his wife!

~~*

When the ceremony was over and the parish book was signed, the couple and their guests set out for Netherfield. Charles and Jane had generously offered to host the wedding breakfast at their home as it had a ballroom large enough to comfortably accommodate the many guests. Elizabeth decided that Miss Bingley refused to come to the wedding because she viewed both Netherfield and Mr. Darcy as belonging to her, and both had been snatched from her grasp. Elizabeth did not believe for one moment that Caroline had taken ill.

When the carriage drove away from the church, Darcy wrapped an arm about Elizabeth, pulling her close to him. "I have never felt such happiness... such abundant hope and joy... as I do now." He played with a lock of her hair and then ran a finger down her cheek. "It has been a long time since I have felt this way."

Elizabeth felt a surge of delight and leaned into his hand. "I could not be happier to hear you say that, as I feel the same."

Their eyes locked for a moment, conveying all the depth of emotion each felt, and then Darcy lowered his head, pressing his lips to hers in a kiss longer and more passionate than any of the ones they had previously shared, and Elizabeth felt their hearts beat in unison. When he finally pulled away, the couple was silent, except for Darcy's heavy breathing.

At length, he said softly, "Tell me, Elizabeth, and be honest. How is your foot?"

She winced. "Did I limp while walking down the aisle? I hoped no one would notice."

Darcy gave his head a quick shake. "I only observed that you were holding your father's arm tightly, and he was holding yours just as firmly. You were beautiful walking down the aisle towards me, so much so, that I was tempted to run to you."

Her expression became thoughtful. "I am glad. I was not in much pain, but I was mindful that I did not wish to stumble."

Elizabeth glanced out the window and then turned her eyes back to him. "I know you are not eager to be in the midst of all the people at the wedding breakfast." She smiled mischievously. "Did you, perchance, give the driver instructions to set out directly for London? You surely remember that he should have turned down that road to Netherfield."

"The thought had crossed my mind, but no. I asked him to take a more indirect route to allow our guests to arrive first." He was silent for a moment, and his smile displayed the depth of his love. "Besides, I wanted to have more time alone with you." He was unable to take his eyes off her.

Elizabeth chuckled. "Mr. Darcy, you simply must stop staring at me. Remember, you will be expected to converse with our wedding breakfast guests."

"On one condition, Elizabeth. *You* simply must start calling me Fitzwilliam, instead of Mr. Darcy!" He gave her a pointed look.

"Oh, but Fitzwilliam is such a long name."

"Long? It is no longer in syllables than Elizabeth!" He let out a huff. "And it sounds shorter than saying Mis-ter Dar-cy. In fact, with the pause between names, it seems as if it were five syllables while Fitz-wil-liam is but three."

Elizabeth laughed and gave a resigned shrug. "All right, Fitzwilliam, it is. But do not be surprised if one day I begin calling you Fitz or Will." She smiled playfully.

He leaned over and kissed her nose, but he was not smiling. "Please do not call me Fitz. It was a name one particular acquaintance of mine – from childhood – called me, and it was usually spoken in a derogatory manner." He lifted a brow. "I will not utter his name, but you know of whom I speak."

Elizabeth felt her insides tighten, and she squeezed his hand.

"Oh, dear, I can understand your aversion to the name." She gave him a loving, reassuring smile. "Then it shall be Will." She paused and then added, "Unless, of course, you are in trouble with me, and then you shall be Fitzwilliam."

He turned on the seat to face her. "And exactly what, my dearest, will get me in trouble for you to call me Fitzwilliam?"

"I can make up a list for you." She smiled teasingly. "There are several things I will not tolerate."

"Such as?"

She began counting on her fingers. "One, taking walks about Pemberley without me." She gave a shrug. "Or for the time being, without a horse readied for me to ride with you."

"Gwendolyn."

"Gwendolyn?"

"Yes, the horse on which Georgiana learned to ride. She is gentle, sturdy, and reliable. What else is on that list of yours?"

"Two, gazing out a window to escape conversation. You may walk over to a window to view the prospect below, but not to avoid conversation. Any conversation... including one with my mother."

Darcy let out a sigh and rolled his eyes. "Your mother?"

"Indeed, and it begins directly. During the wedding breakfast there will be no walking away."

"Duly noted," Darcy said. "And what, pray tell, is number three?"

Elizabeth pondered this and reached up to lightly caress his cheek. "You must greet me each morning with a smile and a kiss, and then end each night with the same."

"Gladly." He grasped her fingers, bringing them to his lips.

"But when I address you as Fitzwilliam Reginald Darcy, you will know that you are seriously in trouble."

He lowered his forehead to touch hers. "And what, pray tell, are the sins I will commit that will prompt the use of my full name?"

She lifted her eyes to him. "Spending hours locked away in your study or library for the sole purpose of avoiding people or... neglecting your children."

"Children?"

Elizabeth smiled. "Certainly."

He gave an assenting nod. "And what else?"

She drew in a deep breath. "Avoiding difficult circumstances while merely hoping they will disappear."

"These would be serious offenses, indeed." Very softly, he asked, "Might I inquire whether these are tendencies you witnessed in your father?"

She turned and looked straight ahead, nodding mutely.

He kissed the top of her head. "I will do my best to please you, Elizabeth."

She looked back at him and smiled. "I know you shall."

"Now, since you have had your say, it is my turn."

Elizabeth sat erect. "I am ready to hear what you have to say, my dear."

His face grew serious. "When I address you as Mrs. Darcy, it shall only be when we are in a large crowd." He drew in a breath. "When I call you Mrs. Darcy, I am telling you that I am in need of your assistance to help me follow the conversation."

Elizabeth dropped her shoulders. "Oh," she replied in almost a sigh. A wave of distress filled her that she had been teasing him, and he had harboured such a deep concern. "I... I can only imagine how difficult this has been for you."

"As I explained before, I have found things I could do to help me in most situations." He tilted his head. "But having you by my side will be all I need from now on."

She stroked his cheek with her hand. "I promise I will always be by your side when you need me... whatever the reason."

"I trust that you will." Darcy glanced out the window. "We have arrived at Netherfield. Are you ready, my dear?"

Elizabeth chuckled. "*I* certainly am, but are *you*?"

Chapter 23

Mrs. Gardiner was the first person Elizabeth saw when she stepped down from the carriage at Netherfield. She walked over to her and wrapped her in a warm embrace. "Hello, dearest Aunt!"

Her aunt leaned in and whispered, "How was your first carriage ride as Mrs. Elizabeth Darcy?"

Elizabeth glanced back at her husband, who was surrounded by Georgiana, Colonel Fitzwilliam, and his family. Looking back at her aunt, she said, "It was delightful. We discussed all aspects of our married life and are convinced we shall never have any trouble."

Mrs. Gardiner laughed. "Oh, Lizzy, would that all marriages be established within the first hour as yours seems to be."

"You cannot know, Aunt, how grateful I am to you for helping to bring about this day."

Mrs. Gardiner placed her hands on her niece's shoulders. "I beg to disagree, Lizzy, as I have observed that Mr. Darcy is a very determined gentleman, and he would have soon contrived a way to bring this about himself, with or without us taking you to town that day you encountered him."

Elizabeth smiled. "Oh, but it is much more than that. You taught me a great deal about how to act and behave as a lady. I would never have mastered it otherwise." She gave her aunt a knowing look and leaned in and kissed her cheek. "For that, I am most grateful."

"Oh, Lizzy, I am certain I deserve no such praise."

"Oh, but you do!" Elizabeth took her aunt's familiar hands and squeezed them. "I had best return to my husband. Again, I thank you for everything!"

"Certainly."

As Elizabeth turned, she felt someone at her side. She glanced over, expecting to see her husband. Instead, it was Georgiana, wearing a broad smile.

The two embraced, and Georgiana said, "I am delighted to welcome you into our family, and I am especially pleased that you are now my sister."

"That means a great deal to me, Georgiana. I feel the same about you."

Georgiana drew back and said, "My brother requests your presence, if you would be so kind, *Mrs. Darcy*." She chuckled. "He told me to specifically say that."

Elizabeth saw that her husband was now surrounded by people from the neighbourhood. She laughed. "It has begun." She walked over to him with great love and admiration, knowing he was relying on her to get him through the remainder of the morning.

~~*

The wedding breakfast was a delightful, joyous affair. Jane had worked diligently with her housekeeper, Mrs. Matthews, to bring about a successful celebration of the marriage of Mr. and Mrs. Darcy.

When the newlywed couple stepped into the ballroom, they were greeted with a beautifully decorated room laden with flowers, lit candles, and tables filled with succulent foods. There was also a larger crowd of people than had been at the ceremony. When Jane and Charles joined them, Elizabeth hugged her sister, thanking her for all she had done for them. She drew back, and the two sisters faced each other with tears pooling in their eyes. While it was a joyous celebration, both were very much aware that it meant the two of them would now be even farther apart from each other.

"Oh, Lizzy! I am so happy for you, but how I shall miss you!" Jane leaned in and whispered, "Charles and I are already talking of finding a home to buy in Derbyshire. It is our dream to live close to you."

"That would be delightful, Jane. I can think of nothing I would like better."

"Do not mention it to anyone." She glanced over at her mother and father. "They will not be pleased. Besides, it will likely take a while to find a suitable home."

"I promise I will not say a word."

As they walked about the room, there were introductions that Elizabeth made, and expressions of appreciation to them for their well-wishes.

She enjoyed every conversation, including Mr. and Mrs. Hurst, who offered their sincere congratulations to the couple. Elizabeth could not help thinking that Caroline was likely the instigator of all the unpleasant remarks made to her, and that Mrs. Hurst was a very amiable person without her sister urging her along.

Mr. and Mrs. Arnold and their nephew approached and wished them great joy. Mrs. Arnold assured Mr. Darcy that she knew from the day Elizabeth was born, that she would one day attract the eye of a fine gentleman and become an excellent wife. She smiled, looking almost as proud as if she were the mother of the bride.

Her nephew then addressed them. "I wish you both great joy and happiness. It has been a delight gaining the acquaintance of you both."

Elizabeth stole a glance at Kitty and then turned back to him. "Perhaps in a short while, you will be the one receiving wishes of joy." She smiled and teasingly lifted a single brow.

He looked over at Kitty, nodding slowly. "Perhaps," he said with a chuckle.

A short while later both Mary and Kitty came up and expressed their congratulations, and after Mary stepped away, Kitty lingered.

"Lizzy, I want to thank you for taking the time to help me grow more confident in myself." She looked at the younger Mr. Arnold. "His parents are coming to Hertfordshire in a few weeks, and he would like me to meet them."

Elizabeth drew her sister into an embrace. "I am delighted, Kitty!"

The sisters talked a little more, and when Kitty walked away, Charles and Jane returned to their side as the breakfast was about to be served. Elizabeth tucked her arm in Jane's as they walked to the table.

Darcy and Elizabeth sat with their closest family. Mr. and Mrs.

Bennet sat across from them, Darcy's sister and the Fitzwilliams sat on his side, and Elizabeth's sisters and Charles sat on her side. Elizabeth was pleased her mother was subdued during the breakfast. In fact, as she reflected on it, she realized her mother had seemed much calmer since learning of her engagement to Mr. Darcy. With the marriages of her two eldest daughters to two gentlemen of good fortune, she likely had fewer worries pressing on her now.

After the breakfast, Lydia came up to Elizabeth and asked if she could speak with her alone. The two found a corner to themselves.

"What is it, Lydia?"

Her youngest sister drew in a long breath. "I want to offer my congratulations to you both, but I also have a confession."

Elizabeth felt a sense of dread pass through her, but she remained calm. "A confession?"

Lydia turned her head and then looked back ruefully. "When I was in Brighton, and I told Mrs. Forster that Wickham was going to run off and wanted me to go with him..."

"Yes?"

"I had decided to go with him."

"Oh, Lydia!"

"I know... I know. But when I saw how concerned she was, and how wrong she said it was, I realized I was being foolish. I then assured her I only told her so Wickham could be stopped before he got in more trouble than he already was, and that I never had any intention of going off with him."

"But you had originally decided differently?"

Lydia's features grew solemn. "Mrs. Forster had no idea that my motive in telling her was to boast about him wanting me to go with him. She thanked me for informing her and said she would let her husband know directly so action could be taken. I pretended I told her so he would be stopped." Lydia dropped her head. "I have never told anyone this, and I have felt so ashamed... and unhappy." She looked up. "You will not tell anyone, please?"

"I will not, Lydia, as long as you promise to never consider doing anything as foolish again!" She drew her sister into her arms. "Thank you for confiding in me." Elizabeth drew back. "Is this why you have seemed so melancholy of late? You have not been your normal exuberant self!"

Lydia wiped a tear that rolled down her cheek. "I feel as though I do not even know how to act." She looked at Kitty. "Kitty has changed so much for the better, and I am at a loss to know how she did it."

Elizabeth smiled. "Lydia, you have two older sisters at home. You can learn a great deal from them."

Lydia's eyes widened, and she drew back sharply. "Even Mary?"

Elizabeth gave her a reassuring nod. "What Mary says usually has truth to it. You may not agree with the way she says it, but there are always nuggets you can glean from her."

Lydia huffed. "I suppose."

"And Kitty has learned a great deal in the past few months, and I daresay you can learn much from her." She took her youngest sister's hands. "And Jane is still nearby. I know that you probably feel that you are vastly different from your sisters, but you can learn from each one."

Lydia squeezed Elizabeth's hands. "Thank you. I will miss you, Lizzy."

"And I will miss you, too, Lydia."

~~*

At length, it was time for the newly married couple to take their leave.

For Darcy, the wedding breakfast had gone on a little longer than he would have preferred, but he was grateful to have had Elizabeth at his side. She seemed to have an innate way of discerning when he needed assistance following the conversation, and she found ways to either answer for him or repeat the question to him in a way that would not draw attention to his hearing deficiency.

For Elizabeth, however, the wedding breakfast had not lasted long enough. She took delight in conversing with her friends and family and introducing her husband to those he had never met. She was amazed that she had not previously noticed the difficulty he had hearing, and it grieved her to realize it was something he had struggled with his entire life.

At length, Darcy and Elizabeth walked out to the carriage after more hugs and farewells. Mr. and Mrs. Bennet followed, as well as Jane and Charles, and Georgiana. Elizabeth turned to say goodbye to her parents. Both had tears glistening in their eyes. She was certain that while her mother's tears were of joy, her father's were more likely due to the fact that he would miss her.

"You both must come to Pemberley," Mr. Darcy said to them. "Or at least visit us in town when we are there."

"Oh, yes!" wailed Mrs. Bennet. "I should very much like to visit you in London. It is not such a long journey as Pemberley."

Mr. Bennet laughed. "And I will be sure to visit you at Pemberley. No distance will keep me from seeing the library I have heard so much about. I would very much like to see it!"

"You both would be most welcome," Darcy said.

"I do hope you will come visit us," Elizabeth said to her parents.

"And you must also visit us!" Mr. Bennet spoke in a manner that was both scolding and teasing. Elizabeth knew, however, that despite his smile, he was sincere. She held and kissed them both.

Jane approached Elizabeth, and the two sisters clasped each other tightly. Elizabeth whispered, "I do hope you and Charles will come to Pemberley soon. We will let you know if we discover any suitable property nearby that comes available."

"Thank you, Lizzy. I will miss you."

"And I will miss you, too!" She kissed her on the cheek, wiping away a tear.

Georgiana stood patiently waiting. She walked up to her brother and hugged him tightly. She then turned to Elizabeth, taking her hands in hers. "I could not be happier, Elizabeth. I know that you have fulfilled my brother's every wish and dream, but you have also fulfilled mine. You are everything I have ever wanted in a sister."

Elizabeth drew her into a close embrace. "I look forward to spending more time with you."

"As do I!" Georgiana exclaimed with a smile.

The couple walked to the waiting carriage, and as Elizabeth was being helped up, she turned back one last time and looked at everyone. She gave them a broad smile before stepping in. Darcy turned back briefly, giving a quick wave, and followed his wife in. As the carriage began to pull away, they waved one last time, knowing they would not soon return, and settled in.

"Well, my dearest Elizabeth, our new journey now begins." He clasped her hands in his. "It is my every hope and prayer that I will be the best of husbands to you and make you eternally happy." He lifted her hands to his lips and kissed them.

She tilted her head and smiled. "I am already happier than I could have ever imagined."

"Elizabeth Rose, your happiness is all that is needed for my happiness."

Elizabeth sent him a quizzical glance. "Elizabeth Rose? You have never called me that." She leaned in to him. "What does this mean when you address me as Elizabeth Rose?"

"Did I not mention it? Hm, it must have slipped my mind." He drew the curtain closed on the window by him, and then reached over to close the curtain on the other side. He looked at her and smiled mischievously.

Before she could question him further, he picked her up and placed her on his lap. He slowly began to remove the flowers and pins from her hair, letting it fall to her shoulders.

Elizabeth shivered as his fingers trailed down her neck, but even more so when he leaned in to kiss the tender area. He wrapped her in his arms and began to speak softly, his breath tickling her ears and warming her down to her toes.

"When I call you by your first and middle name, Elizabeth Rose, there is a remarkably simple answer to what I desire. And yet, it is also a rather complex answer, one I would prefer to show you rather than try to explain."

Elizabeth felt his arms tighten about her. "Yes?" she said softly.

"It is *you*, Elizabeth Rose. I want *you*."

Before she could reply, he kissed her soundly. The trip to London was made with not one glance out the window, nor any pages read of the books they had brought along, and no other care or concern other than their love and devotion to each other.

Epilogue

One Year Later

Darcy and Elizabeth walked arm in arm as they took the path around the lake at Pemberley. It was dusk, and as the days had grown long with the ensuing summer, it was still light outside despite the late hour.

Elizabeth glanced up. "I cannot believe it has been one year since our wedding. So much has changed."

"Indeed, it has." He gave a slight shrug. "Save for my aunt's resolute resentment towards me."

Elizabeth paused, bringing the couple to a stop. "Ah, but I recently heard from Charlotte, and she feels progress is being made."

Darcy tilted his head. "How so?"

Smiling, she replied, "Appealing to his pride, Charlotte was finally able to convince Mr. Collins to recognize what an honour it is that one of his cousins married the illustrious Mr. Darcy."

He rolled his eyes.

"He has now taken it upon himself to appeal to Lady Catherine's sense of Christian duty to extend forgiveness to both of us."

"Has he?"

Elizabeth tugged at his arm and the two proceeded to walk. "I think there is no denying she will do what the good Lord has commanded us all to do."

He walked on in silence, save for a soft murmur.

"Perhaps we will take our first outing with the baby next Easter to Kent." She leaned in. "I cannot imagine she would not welcome us to Rosings with the new heir of Pemberley."

"You are likely correct."

They continued a short distance, and as they turned to walk towards the house, they both looked up. The sun had set behind the ridge at the back of the house, and the sky was painted with a mixture of reds, yellows, and oranges.

"I do not think I will ever grow tired of the sunrises or sunsets here, but I would imagine the prospect of the sunset from atop the ridge is beautiful tonight."

Darcy murmured an affirmative. "One day you shall walk to the top, I am certain." He looked down at her stomach, which was just beginning to show evidence of the new life growing inside. "But now you must wait until after the baby has come. I will not have you attempting your first walk up and then not being able to make the trip down."

Elizabeth sighed. "It calls to me as much as Oakham Mount did."

He took her hand, giving it a pat. "I am not surprised. It is unfortunate the path up was too narrow in places for Gwendolyn to carry you to the top."

She gave a shrug. "I suppose I shall have to wait."

"Are you certain you feel well enough to travel, Elizabeth? You had a few months of nausea, and I would be grieved if you were uncomfortable."

"I believe it has passed. I have felt quite well recently." She turned to him. "I would greatly regret missing Kitty's wedding to Mr. Arnold. Besides, we shall have Charles and Jane with us. If I have need of anything, she will be there to help us."

"I am grateful a suitable home for them was found nearby."

"As am I! And with the two of us anticipating a child within a few months of each other, just think how close those cousins will be!"

"Indeed."

They came to an incline in the path that took them back up to the house, and Darcy gripped her hand tightly.

"My dear, there is no further need for that, as my foot is almost completely pain free and healed. Granted, I do not walk with the elegance and poise of Caroline Bingley, but I am grateful for the physician you had tend to me in London and the advice he gave."

"I knew he would know what to do." He shook his head. "And you walk perfectly, without fault!"

Elizabeth laughed. "Hardly! Around others, I am more mindful of each step I take, but around you, I confess I rarely think about it."

He patted her hand. "I am glad. I would not have it any other way."

"Are you ready to face Georgiana's coming out this season with the vaunted Darcy reserve?"

Darcy grunted. "I am not so concerned for the actual presentation at court and the grand ball afterwards, but I have misgivings when I consider all the young men who will pursue her." He kicked the ground with his boot. "I shall be an ogre."

Elizabeth laughed. "Perhaps *she* is the one who ought to have some misgivings."

"I would prefer all the *young men* have misgivings!"

She smiled and leaned her head against his shoulder. "I wrote to Mrs. Cryderman at the bookstore about our expected little one." She gave her stomach a pat. "I knew she would be delighted to hear."

Darcy laughed. "She will likely put aside every child's book that comes in for us to look at when we stop in again."

Elizabeth chuckled. "I hope she does. Our little girl will grow to love reading as much as I do."

Darcy let out a huff. "Do you not mean our little *boy*? He will devour books much like I do – and your father!"

Elizabeth nodded. "Yes, he will." She let out a long sigh.

"Is anything wrong, Elizabeth? Is it your foot?"

"No, nothing is wrong. I am just a little more tired than usual. My foot is certainly much improved over the past year, but I think when we get inside, I will need to rest my feet on several cushions. Perhaps I will read a little."

Darcy's eyes twinkled. "Would it help if I rubbed your feet while you read?"

"That sounds wonderful, but..." She turned to her husband, sending him a teasing, scolding look. "I do not think I will get any reading done with you so near and your passionate attention to my feet, ankles, and..."

"The doctor did suggest it may help."

She shook her head with a laugh. "He did, but you know very well what that often leads to..."

"I do, indeed." He paused to wrap his arms about her and leaned close to kiss her. "If you are willing, then I certainly am." He touched his forehead to hers. "Is that something that might interest you, Elizabeth Rose?"

Elizabeth sighed deeply and smiled. "I do believe I could be easily persuaded."

~ THE END ~

ABOUT THE AUTHOR

Kara Louise grew up in the San Fernando Valley in Southern California, but now lives in the suburbs of St. Louis, Missouri with her husband, and their ever-changing number of birds, dogs, and cats. Their son, his wife, and their three daughters live nearby, so her time is often spent being 'Nana' to them.

Other books by Kara Louise:

Darcy's Voyage
Only Mr. Darcy Will Do
Assumed Engagement
Assumed Obligation
Drive and Determination
Master Under Good Regulation
Pemberley Celebrations: The First Year
Pirates and Prejudice
Mr. Darcy's Rival
A Peculiar Engagement
Chance and Circumstance
and
Mr. Darcy's Magpie

~~*

www.karalouise.net

www.ingramcontent.com/pod-product-compliance
Lightning Source LLC
Chambersburg PA
CBHW031138130726
47988CB00006B/2422